THE UNCERTAIN JOURNEY OF LOVE AND MARRIAGE

A novel by

Ty Waller

Young Dreams Publications

ISBN-10: 0692350691

ISBN-13: 978-0692350690

Young Dreams Publications

Ty Waller is an author for Young Dreams Publications

Young Dreams Publications, CEO & Founder, Ty Waller

Lansing, IL 60438

tywaller@youngdreamsbig.com

info@youngdreamsbig.com

www.youngdreamsbig.com

PREFACE

This novel, *The Uncertain Journey of Love and Marriage* was written from a place of encouragement. I want to remind everyone that reads this novel to remember that no matter how terrible your situation may appear that you must never give up on God. Although this novel has a marriage theme, I believe everyone, regardless of their current relationship status, will be able to relate to the test of faith and the struggles that these characters endured. We live in a world that brings trials and tribulations – this is something that even the Bible says we can't avoid. Sometimes our tribulations will cause us to make the wrong decisions. And likewise, our trials may even cause us to get into a lifestyle that is not pleasing to God and often will bring more pain in our lives than pleasure.

I, too, went through the uncertain journey of love and marriage - it wasn't an easy journey. God showed me many valuable things during the journey, but the most valuable lesson I learned was that if I don't throw away my confidence in Him, He will reward me greatly for it. The reward I received is that I'm stronger in Him, now, than I could have ever imagined and I still have my robe of righteousness.

I hope everyone enjoys this novel. Be blessed!

~Ty Waller

DEDICATIONS

I dedicate this novel to God for being my Rock on which I stand.

I also dedicate this novel to the people who prayed for me during one of the hardest times I ever had to face in my life – they know who they are.

Young Dreams Publications

Chapter 1

Every Tuesday, Wednesday, and every other weekend I come home to this big empty house! Aijah thought as she enters into her newly decorated home from a long evening at the shop. Aijah's clientele had really picked up ever since Lenox and the shop, All About You, appeared on a BET reality show highlighting the best dressed athletes and celebrities, and the people who worked the magic on them. Aijah has gained some notable clientele styling them and doing their nails, in addition to still working full time at the shop. With so much going on she hadn't had a chance to really reflect on what was going on in her personal life.

On this particular Wednesday her son's toy truck, which she stubbed her toe on, jilted her back to the reality of her situation. She picked up Jason's toy, went to his room and placed it in the toy chest. As she looked around the room her eyes came to the picture of Anthony that was posted on Jason's bedroom wall across from his bed. This was one of the pictures left in the house of Anthony – all the others, except for a wedding picture in her den, Aijah took down because she didn't want to be reminded of him. Giving herself a second to breathe, Aijah fell to the floor and sobbed. She had buried herself in her job and didn't allow herself to deal with her personal life. She sobbed seven months' worth of anger, guilt, confusion, unanswered questions, and great sorrow.

For Aijah it was much easier for her to ignore life and focus on work and the Lord. The Lord was really the only thing holding Aijah up over the tragedy of her four-year long marriage. On the day of Aijah and Anthony's fourth year anniversary Anthony didn't come home. Aijah had been sitting home for hours waiting on him to come home so they could go to dinner to celebrate and he never showed up. She was calling his phone but no answer. She would text him but no answer. She called his friends to see if they heard from him but no one had heard from him.

It wasn't until the next morning after the anniversary day that Anthony stumbled into the house at 7:00 am. He was visibly still slightly intoxicated – presumably from the previous night. She couldn't believe what was going on. Aijah remembers going from scared thinking the worst to being so overcome with rage that she wanted to put her hands around Anthony's throat and strangling him to death. She remembers jumping off the sofa where she'd fallen asleep waiting on him to come home. The unlocking of the front door awakened her and she immediately ran to the front door.

"Where have you been, Anthony??!!" Aijah screamed.

Anthony walks through the door and had nothing to say. He walks to the family room and plopped down on the sofa, Aijah sits down next to him, they both stared into each other's eyes not saying a word.

"So, where have you been and why do you look like you're drunk?" Aijah asks again.

"This is not working. I think its best that we separate." Anthony says coldly.

Aijah was stunned and her mouth couldn't speak any words. She knew they had been having some issues but she had no idea they were that serious to cause Anthony to consider separation. Aijah knew that she had been working a lot lately and her home life was suffering, but she had no idea that she was on the brink of losing her family.

"It's not you – you're a great woman but I just can't give you what you need right now. You deserve more than what I can offer you right now." Anthony stood up from off the sofa and went into the guest bedroom.

Aijah laughed out loud, she couldn't believe what she was hearing. She thought she was imagining what had transpired before her eyes. After sitting and really thinking about what was going on she screamed out, "The blood of Jesus!" She stormed to the guest bedroom where Anthony was found lying across the bed.

"No, we're going to talk about this." She said as she sat on the bed next to him.

3

"Aijah let it go. You know we've been having issues lately and there's no need to drag this thing out and put Jason in the middle of it."

"There is nothing too hard for God to work out. No, let's talk about it." Aijah pleaded.

"Look, I don't love you any more, haven't for a while now. I love you because of what we've had in the past and because you're the mother of my son, but let's just stop trying to keep something together that's not working."

The coldness from Anthony was too heart piercing for Aijah to stand. Anthony's dismissive reaction made her steaming mad. Her eyes grew big and eyebrows raised, she jumped off the bed with fierceness. "Well fine if that's how you really feel you can pack your bags and leave my house today. You don't have to wait."

"Ok." Anthony said without hesitation.

Aijah scoffed at his callousness. She stormed out of the room slamming the door behind her.

Aijah sat in the middle of Jason's bedroom reflecting on that tragic morning. She never expected that seven months later they would still be in the space of separation. Anthony had eventually moved into an apartment loft after spending a month and a half as a guest/resident of the Hilton hotel. They had come to a mutual agreement on times they would split between keeping Jason – Anthony would get him every Tuesday and Wednesday, and they would split every other

4

weekend. They decided to go half on all expenses related to Jason and daycare fees.

For the past seven months Aijah had been married to her job and focusing her attention on being a mother, she didn't have time to think about the foolish behavior of her "stupid husband" as she referred to him. She gave it to God and moved on. Her career was taking off in ways that she couldn't even imagine. The marital hiatus gave her the guts to move her career in an area that she had to step out on faith to accomplish. She wanted to open up her own nail salon and spa. Giving posh and high-end services to clientele to help ease and soothe their minds from all that they were going through.

Like most professionals in the beauty industries they become pseudo-counselors to their clients. Most clients tell their beauticians and nail technicians some of their most private issues – and she wanted her business to reflect that atmosphere. Aijah picked herself off the floor and moved along with her evening gathering her thoughts together to go on with her business plan and life. Besides, Jason was coming home the next day, it was her weekend to keep him. Aijah didn't want to bring that unhappy spirit in her household, but wanted it to be filled with love.

Chapter 2

"So how have you been?" Ahlesha whispered to Aijah as she sat at Aijah's station to get her nails done.

The shop was filled to capacity as the patrons were waiting to get cut and styled by the best in Chicago. Ahlesha was trying to make sure she kept her tone low so that there were no ear-hustlers listening in.

"Girl, I'm good. I'm walking on water." Aijah says too casually for Ahlesha to stand.

"Girl, you've been saying that for months. But I know you not as cool about this as you try to make it seem."

Aijah stopped in the middle of filing Ahlesha's nail, "Ahlesha, what you want to do, roll over and die 'cause my husband left me?" She starts back to filing her nail.

Ahlesha laughed, "No, I'm not saying that, but dang can you show some emotion. At least if I saw you shed a tear at least I will know you're human."

"The Bible says cast all my cares upon the Lord. So that's what I'm doing."

"Uhm, God also knows we're human. He won't get mad at you if you cried about it."

Aijah stares into Ahlesha's eyes, "Look, I'm not the first woman whose man left them. You preached to me for so long about getting stronger in the Lord, and now that I am it's like you can't handle it. Life has to go on. I love Anthony, but my life doesn't stop because he's choosing not to be with his family anymore."

"Ok, I digress. I get it. You want to put on this little show for him. You don't want him to see you weak. Ok, I'll go along with this show."

Aijah just shook her head, she wasn't trying to put on a show but was trying not to let her anger and hurt over take her. Yes, Aijah cried when she was alone, but she also prayed to God that he would fix her marriage. For the first three months Aijah would pray every day for God to send Anthony back home, but as the time went by she slowly started to drift away from praying for him to come home. Her prayers for Anthony now were for him to just be covered under the blood. He had shown on many occasions that he had moved on and the more time went by the more Aijah felt that things were over.

Aijah would have her moments when she would call Anthony and try to get him to talk about the marriage and him coming back home. But doing so would only break her down to where she couldn't sleep and she would be up for hours talking herself out of going to the liquor store to buy something to ease her mind and heart – sometimes prayer just didn't feel like it was working. Anthony had turned into such a cold-hearted person, someone she didn't know or recognize. All Anthony was worried about was picking up his son on the days that he was scheduled to get him and nothing more.

But soon, the more Anthony rejected Aijah to more she developed a thick skin about the situation. The more she was rejected the more she began to see a life without him.

As Aijah finished Ahlesha's nails she scrambled around to get her things together. She was running late to meet with one of her clients. She landed a stylist consultant contract with a local news network, Channel 9 News. After seeing the shop on BET and seeing some of Aijah's styling skills they sought after her for consulting. She would dress the anchors and every now and then they would let her host and be a commentator for some of the style segments.

Aijah was finding herself very busy and she would realize that weeks would go by without her thinking about Anthony until someone would bring it up – like Ahlesha did that day at the shop.

Aijah sped to the network as she didn't want to be late in getting the next anchor ready for the 5:00 pm broadcast. Today was very special, this particular anchor was interviewing a well-known entertainment lawyer, who just so happened to ask that Aijah style him personally as well. When Aijah arrived she was greeted by the broadcast director, Betty, who was eager to introduce Aijah to this important interviewee.

"Hey, Aijah. Glad you could make it." Betty was a short, plump, older white lady. Betty stood about five feet tall, Aijah felt like a giant standing next to her, although she wasn't much taller, standing only at five feet six inches. Betty was decked in a mint-green vintage Chanel suit with matching pumps. She looked like she was in charge and everyone else knew it, too.

"Thanks for inviting me, Betty. I was shocked when you told me that I had a personal request for styling other than Lisa."

"Well, you know you've made a name for yourself in Chicago. You're becoming a hot commodity – you really should think about getting an assistant you're becoming almost impossible to reach these days."

"Yes, Betty I know! But I'm such a control freak I don't know if I'm ready to let someone in my life that way."

"Well, you better think of something because you don't want to lose out on important opportunities because you're too busy to return a phone call…" Betty gave Aijah a wink and smirk. "Come on let's get going so that we don't run out of time before the start of the show."

Betty and Aijah rush down the corridor of the news room to the studio set. They run into Lisa who was sitting at the make-up and hair station going over her newscast script for that evening's news.

Lisa Kohls was one of the top female news anchors in Chicago. She also had another accomplishment; she was one of only three Black, female lead news anchors anchoring a prime-time news broadcast. She was tall, had coco-brown smooth skin, and long flowing hair. She was still in her robe as she was waiting on Aijah to get there to go over looks for the evening.

"Hi, Lisa!" Aijah shouting loudly, as she and Lisa had begun to form a very close relationship over the months of her consultation contract.

"Hey, hun!" Lisa stood to give Aijah a big hug. "So what are we having me to wear tonight?"

Aijah begun to walk over to the rack of clothing that was a few steps away from the hair and make-up station. Aijah fumbled through a few looks. "What's the topic for your interview? What are some of the topics in the newscast?"

"Tonight is a light night. We're going to have some fun with the newscast. Since we're having a mild week we'll be discussing some local events in the city and covering the presidential story of the Obama's attending's Sasha's eight-grade graduation."

"Okay…let's see." Aijah goes back-and-forth between two looks that she felt were appropriate. "Okay we'll go with this." Aijah pulls from the rack a white, button-down silk blouse and a red and black, striped pencil skirt. She also picked up some black leather stilettos.

"Yes, I like!" Lisa said with a huge smile on her face.

"Okay, now that you're all set, who is this gentleman that I'm supposed to be styling?"

Betty, who was sitting off to the side, immediately jumped to her feet. "Oh my, let me go and get him out the green room." Betty races away.

Aijah fumbles around through some of the other women's clothing. She began to look around the studio for the rack of men's clothing as she didn't know anything about the man she would be styling that day. Suddenly she hears Betty and a gentleman with a very deep voice approaching them.

Aijah turns around to see who the mystery man was. She recognized him immediately, Calvin Perkins. Calvin was tall, light-skinned, and slim. He was a very polished man with a full beard and Caesar-haircut with deep waves, dressed in a dark grey suit. Calvin had come to the shop a few times to get his hair cut when his regular barber was unavailable. Aijah never had a personal conversation with him other than the "hello" and "good-bye" when he would come to the shop. She was surprised to see that it was him who asked for the styling.

"Hi, Calvin!" Aijah smiled and extended her hand to shake his hand.

"Oh, you two know each other?" Betty said puzzled.

"No, not exactly Betty." Calvin said in his husky deep voice. "I've visted the shop she works at on occasion, that's all."

"Oh, ok. Well I guess I'll don't have to do a formal introduction. Well I leave you in her hands, she's the best." Everyone smiles at each other and Betty walks off.

"Okaaayyyy, so what look are you going for this evening?" Aijah says nervously.

"Actually, I was going to just wear this." Calvin says as he grabs the lapels of his suit jacket and flares them out.

Aijah chuckles. "If you were going to just wear what you came to the studio in, why request my services?"

"Let's just say that this is my way of finding a way to talk to you outside of the shop and other circles we frequent each other in."

"What do you mean by other circles?" Aijah gave him a side-eye.

"Well you probably don't notice me, but I notice you whenever the shop goes to some of the A-list events around the city."

"Oh...so you're a stalker?" Aijah says seriously.

"Oh, no. Don't take it the wrong way." Calvin began to fumble over his words.

Aijah laughs out loud. "No, I'm just playing."

Calvin regains his composure and relaxes as he realizes Aijah was indeed messing with him.

The two keep chatting for a while as Aijah waited for Lisa to get dressed. Aijah's mind was completely somewhere else as she didn't realize the entire time that Calvin was flirting with her. The broadcast went on without a hitch and the evening ended with Aijah giving Calvin her card to call her whenever he had a real consulting job for her.

Chapter 3

Aijah was in a good mood this particular morning. She had taken the day off to spend some much needed quality time with Jason. Aijah had been so busy that her two-year old was growing up right before her eyes and she was missing out on all the important parts of his development. Aijah was spot cleaning the house as she was waiting on Anthony to bring Jason home that morning from having him on Tuesday and Wednesday.

Aijah was busying herself around the house when she heard keys unlocking her front door. *Girl, you need to build up the courage to tell him to give you the keys to your house back.* Aijah walked to the front door. Jason ran into the house yelling, "Mommmmmyyyyy!!" He had a humongous smile on his face, Aijah did too as she was happy to see her son.

"Hey my baby!" Aijah scooped up the little toddler and began to give him an abundance of hugs and kisses. After she was done showering Jason with love, her smile turned to a frown as she laid eyes on Anthony.

Some days Aijah would be in love with Anthony, and others she would hate his guts - this day she hated his guts.

Her emotions for him were just like PMS symptoms; her like for him depended on what time of the month it was.

"Hi, Anthony." Aijah said in a disgusted tone.

"Hey, how are you today?" Anthony always seemed happy. To Aijah, Anthony always appeared as if he was just living the life he always wanted aside from Aijah. She never sensed any wanting or desire from Anthony. Aijah always looked for the smallest sign from Anthony to see if there was still any love in his heart for her – she never could find one ounce. It hurt her to the core to see that he simply had gone on with his life without her, while she was still praying for a life with him.

"I'm just fine, just fine." Aijah said sarcastically.

"What's your problem?" Anthony asked.

"Nothing."

"Are you sure?"

Aijah didn't say a word she just stood there for a few second staring at Anthony. After a few more seconds she spoke, "When are you going to give me the keys to my house back?"

Anthony snickered. "Keys to your house? You mean keys to *our* house?"

"No I mean keys to *my* house. You abandoned me, remember? So love don't live here anymore."

"Oh here we go with this victim mess. When are you going to get over this?"

Aijah fought to hold back tears. Anthony's coldness could cut her like a knife at times. No matter how much she tried to be strong in his presence. Anthony still had her heart, and the rejection was hard to tolerate at times.

"Dang, you just really don't love me anymore? After all this time, you don't miss me, have anything for me?" Aijah was pleading her heart out. She went from anger, asking for her keys, to melting right in front of him.

"Nope…" Anthony said emotionlessly.

Aijah's heartache turned into rage immediately. "You are one cold-hearted man. I can't believe I married a man like you."

"Well we live and we learn, don't we?"

Aijah was stunned. By now you would think that she would be used to Anthony's cold-heartedness. Somewhere in her heart she was still wishing for a change to come about, but her wishes seemed to go unanswered from God. Aijah would pray and beg God to send her husband back home. It seemed the more and more she prayed, the more Anthony grew more distant.

"I don't know what happened to you. You let this world get ahold of you and now you're a different man – such a different man from the one that I married."

"Well…" Anthony began to speak but Aijah cut him off.

"Look, I just want you to give me my keys back. I don't like the fact that you can just come in here whenever you feel like it. I don't have keys to your house."

"Well when you want to pay this mortgage and all the other expenses that comes along with this house, then I'll be happy to give you *your* keys back, but until then I'll come and go as I please." Anthony began to walk toward Jason's room to tell him good-bye. "Anyway, you're beginning to make more money than me anyway so I don't know why I'm still paying for this house."

"You're paying for this house because it's still your obligation. You left, I didn't force you out."

"Hey Jason, come give daddy a hug good-bye." Anthony said ignoring Aijah.

Jason came running toward Anthony, "Bye, Daddy." They both hugged each other tightly.

As Anthony was walking toward the door to leave he turns to Aijah, "You want your keys back?"

"Yes!" Aijah says anxiously thinking Anthony was going to give them back at that moment.

"Then divorce me!" Anthony walks out the door.

Aijah was stuck standing there watching him walk to his car to get into his black, luxury sedan. Aijah shook her head and slams her front door as she watches him drive off.

Chapter 4

"So you're on his side for leaving." Ahlesha asks Sean.

Sean and Ahlesha were getting ready to go to a Black Ensemble play they and Aijah and Anthony committed to prior to the separation of Aijah and Anthony.

"No, Ahlesha." Sean sighs in frustration to Ahlesha's snarky tone. "I'm just saying, you don't know everything that happens in their household so don't judge the situation."

"Oh…and I guess you got the inside scoop. You're just the fly on the wall, huh?" Ahlesha says snapping and rolling her neck.

"Look! I'm just saying, don't go to this theater acting all crazy and looking at Anthony like you want to cut his manhood off. You don't know what happen and why he left, he may have a good reason. Let's just pray for them and stay out of it."

"Yeah, whatever. Aijah is my sister and it just hurts me that Anthony just up and left their marriage like that." Ahlesha's tone went from upset to hurt. "You remember when we all first got married? Anthony was so happy, I wonder what happen?"

"Baby, life is what happened. Don't go trying to fix nobody else's marriage, worry about your own." Sean flinched as he said that.

"What?!" Ahlesha turned quickly from putting on her makeup, like in the scene from *Waiting to Exhale* when Angela Bassett's character's husband told her he was leaving her.

Sean laughed out loud and quickly tried to clean up his comment. "Naw, baby, I didn't mean it like that. I'm just saying we need to stay out of their business and just focus on us. You know how spirits like to jump from one situation to another. I don't want us to start arguing and stuff and then you be like Anthony and try to leave me."

Ahlesha pursed her lips, "Uhm-hmm." She turned back to the mirror to finish her makeup.

****

There was silence in the car as Aijah and Anthony rode on the way to the theatre. They both tried their best to get out of going, but Sean and Ahlesha purposely couldn't find a replacement for the two tickets. They figured if they forced them to spend some time together than maybe it would help spark something back up in the marriage.

Although Aijah was reluctant to go on the "date" she made sure she was looking fabulous. Although she knows the Bible says that the way to draw a man is with a meek and quiet spirit, she knew it didn't hurt if she added a little sex appeal to it as well. She wore a hot pink, knee-length, bandage dress with her nude stiletto sandals.

When they finally arrived to the theater, Anthony parked the car, and still being the gentleman he walked to the other side and opened Aijah's door to let her out.

"Thank you." Aijah said quietly as she got out the car.

Anthony tried his hardest not to stare, but he couldn't help it as his eyes roamed the curves of her body.

Aijah caught a glimpse of Anthony staring. "Well since you can't keep your eyes off me you might as well say how good I look."

Anthony scoffs at Aijah, "Girl, I wasn't looking at you. But since you brought it up, step back and let me look at you."

Anthony gave Aijah a good once over as he walked around her in a circle. "You look aight..."

"Whatever." Aijah says as she lightly slaps him across the head and walks away. Anthony watches her butt as she walks away.

As they walk into the theatre lobby they spot Sean and Ahlesha sitting waiting for them. Sean spots them and taps Ahlesha and points in Aijah and Anthony's direction.

They both stand to greet the couple, everyone exchanges hugs and they walk into the mezzanine to grab their seats. When they get to their four seats, the two ladies sit on the inside and the men sat outside of them accordingly. They had some small talk until the lights started going down at the start of the show.

The theme of the play couldn't have been more ironic, the play was entitled, *Love is like a Love Song*. The stage play took some of the most heart-felt, heart-wrenching love songs from the early 50's to the 90's, and set them as the soundtrack to two lovers going in and out of love.

The opening scene started out with the lovers meeting and the theme song was "Come and Talk to Me" by Jodeci. It was a nostalgic moment for Aijah as it took her back to the moment that she met Anthony. The day she met him she was at the pharmacy picking up some cough medicine for a cold that she had - he was there for the same reason. They both hit it off while talking about what brands worked and what didn't work, and they ended up exchanging numbers.

The play continued on with a love song medley that mirrored the two lovers' budding romance. "Could It Be I'm Falling in Love" by the Spinners; "La La Means I Love You" by The Delfonics; and "Crusin'" by Smokey Robinson were the first round of songs that melodically showed their growing love.

Then the romance began to evolve as the lovers moved into more intimate territory: "Just To Be Close To You" by the Commodores; "Your Body's Callin'" by R. Kelly; & "Tonight is the Night" by Betty Wright.

During the more intimate scenes Aijah and Anthony slowly gravitated toward one another – Anthony even put his arm around Aijah as they somewhat snuggled while watching the scenes. Sean and Ahlesha were sure to notice as they both smiled at the couple, thinking that some reconciliation was going to take place.

However, a love song themed play wouldn't be right without the inevitable make up to break up songs. The two lovers' happy romance began to turn sour - and there was great music to follow: "Get It Together" by 702; "Brokenhearted" by Brandy; "Not Gon' Cry" by Mary J. Blige; and "Love TKO" by Teddy Pendergrass. The emotion was so high during the break up scenes that Aijah and Anthony began to drift apart slowly. Aijah began to feel all the hurt she felt from Anthony leaving her that day after their anniversary. The lyrics from the songs expressed every sentiment that was bottleed up inside, she silently allowed the songs to speak for her. She had to catch herself from shedding tears as she viewed the two lovers serenade one another on the stage.

But fortunately this play had a happy ending; the two lovers would find their way back to love in the end with a heart-felt medley: "Wish I Didn't Miss You" by Angie Stone; "I Can't Sleep" by R. Kelly; "Let's Stay Together" by Al Green; and "Let's Get Married" by Jagged Edge. Then the curtains went down, light were up, and Aijah found herself nestled right back in the nook of Anthony's armpit. She had to shake herself back to the reality of their current situation – Anthony did too.

As they were driving back home in the awkward silence Aijah had no clue what to say, and neither did Anthony. When they arrived back to Aijah's house Anthony got out to walk Aijah to the door. Aijah's heart began to beat profusely as she was unsure if Anthony was going to invite himself in or not – she was hoping he would. It had been going eight months since Aijah had sex. Aijah kept her body holy during her and Anthony's separation, she treasured her body being the temple of God and didn't want to defile it with adultery. Aijah was desperately hoping that Anthony would put out the fire that was burning in her flesh.

When they got to the door Aijah didn't want to leave anything to chance so she took matters into her own hands. "Hey, you wanna come in?" She said sensually.

Anthony paused for a moment, and then he hesitantly spoke, "I don't think it will be a good idea."

"Why not?!" Aijah asked puzzled. Anthony just stood there. Seeing that she felt he needed a little coaxing she grabbed Anthony by his shirt and pulled him close to her and tried to kiss him.

He pulled his head back and backed away from Aijah. Aijah was really confused now.

"Anthony what's going on with you?"

"I think this would be a mistake if we did this." He gave Aijah a hug and walked away to his car.

Aijah was left standing dumbfounded, she just knew Anthony was going to give in to her sexual advances, as sexy as she was that night what man would turn her down?

She watched Anthony as he drove off. *Ok, either he's gay, has a girlfriend, or just doesn't want me anymore.* Aijah thought as she tried to figure out the reasoning for Anthony's rejection. But she became conflicted as she reflected on how Anthony snuggled up to her while they were at the theater.

She went in her home and took a hot shower to try to get her mind off of the situation – she had gotten her hormones all bubbled up and now she had to cool them down.

Chapter 5

"This place is perfect! It looks really nice. What's the rent on this every month?" Aijah asks the realtor of a business space she was looking into. With her clientele picking up and her consultation business picking up, Aijah decided it was time to step out on faith and embark on her dream of owning her own nail spa.

"Well you will be getting it at the bargain price of $5,000 a month." The sharply dressed realtor said.

"Wow, Marko, the bargain price of $5,000, huh? Will the owner build to suit?" Aijah says.

"We can check on that for you, but I'm sure he will have no problem doing whatever you need – seeing that we have a local celebrity bringing big business to the South Loop area."

"Ok great, Marko! I'm ready to sign the lease whenever we get everything finalized. He wants first and last months, as well as a $7,000 security deposit, right?"

"Yes!" Marko says.

"Ok, well when the papers are drawn up I'll have the cashier's check ready for him. I would love to have a September opening!"

"Ok. I'll speak with the owner and get right on it."

They both hugged each other and went their separate ways. Aijah was chipper about the journey she was about to take as a business owner, but that chipperness soon turned into anxiety. She realized that it would soon be time to confirm to Lenox that she was going to be leaving the shop.

Aijah leaving the shop shouldn't be a surprise to Lenox, Aijah had been hinting around to it as she had been noticing she was becoming too busy to have normal appointments. But Lenox was controlling and he liked to have the final say in everything, even if it was someone else's business.

Aijah finally arrives at the shop and immediately she felt the anxiety. She was a grown woman, but talking to Lenox about anything was sometimes no easy task. As she walks into the shop she finds it packed to capacity as usual. She spots Lenox speaking to some clients and she proceeds to head in his direction.

"Hey, baby sister!" Lenox says with a big smile as he greets Aijah.

"Hey, big bro." They hug.

Over the years their friendship had grown so close that they saw each other as brother and sister.

"Hey, when you get a chance I need to speak to you about something." Aijah says hesitantly.

Lenox's smile turned into a slight frown. "What's going on?"

"Nothing. I just need to talk to you about something." Aijah responds back.

"Ok. Well let's talk now. I don't have any clients for the rest of the day."

Aijah sighs slightly and they both go on to walk to Lenox's office. Lenox had redecorated nicely. He had put in a new all cherry wood desk and credenza. He also had a modern looking, leather executive office chair, with stainless steel finishing on the arm rests. He also had matching guest seating to match. His office definitely looked like the office of a successful high-profile business owner.

Lenox sits down in his chair and Aijah sits down in one of the guest seats.

"So what's up?" Lenox says.

"Well you know business has been picking up for me. And with all of my clientele I have coming in and out of the shop, it is evident that I'm growing out of the space."

Lenox leans back in his seat as he suspects the news that Aijah is about to lay on him.

Aijah continues. "So I went and looked at a space today and I'm going to sign a lease and open up my own nail salon and spa."

Aijah almost cringes as she sits and waits for Lenox's response. He just sat there and looked at Aijah for a while. Aijah began to get a little irritated at his speechlessness.

She bucks her eyes at Lenox, shrugs her shoulders and lifts her hands. "Well are you going to say something?"

Lenox lets out a loud laugh, which startled Aijah. "I'm so proud of you!"

Aijah lets out a sigh of relief and smiles. "Ok. Great!"

Lenox still laughing. "I wanted you to think I was mad. I know y'all think y'all know me around her. But ole' Lenox always have tricks up his sleeve."

Lenox gets up and comes from around the desk to give Aijah a big hug. "So when do you plan on opening this shop?" He says as he begins to pull away from Aijah.

"I'm hoping to have it open in September."

"Wow, September, huh?" Lenox says as he sits back down.

"Yes, September. I'm just waiting on the realtor to get back to me so that I can sign the lease."

"Ok. Well have you come up with a name yet?"

"Yes I have." Aijah smiles

"Well..." Now Lenox was waiting on Aijah to respond.

"I'm going to call it Posh Studios. You like it?"

Lenox shakes his head and begins to stroke his chin hairs. "Yeeaaahhhh. I think that sounds really upscale. I see big bro has taught you well."

"Yes, I learn from the best. You're not the most popular urban barbershop in Chicago for nothing."

"Yeah, you got that right!"

Aijah was relieved that the conversation had went so well. She didn't need the stress of Lenox's disappointment, while she was on a four month deadline to opening up the spa.

Aijah walked out of the office to take care of the four walk-in clients who were so patiently waiting for her, now known, celebrity skills. She loved this new journey of her career.

Chapter 6

"So, man, do you think you're going to go back home?" Sean asked Anthony.

The two of them had met up for coffee at a local coffee shop. Sean had been worried about Anthony. Sean also wanted to get some more information, for himself, about why Anthony left – and for Ahlesha because she was wearing Sean out talking about it almost every other day.

"Naw. I think it's for the best that I stay away. Aijah and I have been having a few issues, anyway." Anthony says.

"You don't think if you talk to her and tell her what's going on that she'll be understanding?"

Anthony curled his lips and shook his head no. "Man with the way that I left, it don't matter how I come to Aijah she wouldn't receive me. I acted out of frustration when I left. I wasn't thinking clearing, I was still intoxicated the next morning. The damage was already done so I just decided to keep rolling with it."

"Well, she is a woman of God, I know she has some forgiveness in her heart for you, somewhere." Sean said unconvincingly.

Anthony laughed. "Man, you don't even believe that yourself. It's just done, man. Let's just leave it alone."

"Well what about Jason?"

"Well let's just say thank God Aijah didn't turn into one of those stupid women that use the child to get back at the father for the failed relationship. It would kill me if she didn't let me see Jason, especially considering the circumstances."

Sean shook his head in agreement to what Anthony was saying.

Anthony continued. "I'm trying to spend as much time as I can with him, though. He's my heart." Tears began to well-up in Anthony's eyes. He was heartbroken at the dissolution of his family. "How could this have happen? This wasn't the life that I chose." Anthony spoke through a cracking voice with unshed tears in his eyes.

Sean looked upon his friend with deep sadness in his eyes. He didn't know what to say or do. All he could offer to Anthony was prayer and faith in God. His friend had lost his faith, was losing his family, and was broken down beyond repair.

****

"I talked to Anthony today." Sean says to Ahlesha later that evening while eating dinner.

"Oh really! What the bum say?" Ahlesha says with distain of the mentioning of Anthony's name.

Sean shook his head. "Ahlesha, you don't even know the circumstances of the situation. Don't judge before you have full knowledge."

Ahlesha was thrown off by Sean's reaction to her reaction. "Unless he has a very good reason for leaving his wife and son, don't tell me not to judge."

"I don't even know why I told you that I spoke with him. You know sometimes you act like you don't have any type of God in you. Apostle Paul says, 'Judge nothing before the time.' God will bring all things to light in due time."

Ahlesha scoffed. "You almost made me say something I couldn't take back. And since you quoting Bible verses, Jesus also said it's unlawful to put away your wife." Ahlesha begins to point her fork at Sean, moving it in a conducting manner. "So like I said, unless he as a good reason for leaving his wife and son - DON'T. TELL. ME. NOT. TO. JUDGE!"

Ahlesha throws the fork down on her plate and gets up from the table. Sean acts as if he's not fazed by Ahlesha's little temper tantrum. Sean then looked at Maurice and Sean, Jr., who were both looking on at their parents as if they were watching a tennis match between Serena and Venus Williams.

"Don't mind your mother. She's just worried about Auntie Aijah and Uncle Anthony." He says with a smile. The two young boys laugh and continue to eat their dinner. They were too young to understand the nature of the conversation anyhow.

Ahlesha was beginning to feel a certain way about Sean's defending of Anthony. Sean was a honorable man of God. How was he appearing to seem "ok" with Anthony leaving his family? Ahlesha could understand why Sean's reaction was making her feel insecure. They, too, had been having some marital issues and she wasn't sure that if Sean's reaction was his outward showing that he may be contemplating leaving, too.

Ahlesha rushes back to the dinner table from out of the bedroom, were she retreated to. "And if you're thinking about leaving, too, there's the door. You and Anthony can get y'all a two bedroom apartment and be roommates."

Sean laughed out loud and threw his hands in the air. "What?! Where did that come from?"

"I mean, since you're in such agreement with Anthony leaving. Do you secretly wish you were leaving, too?" Ahlesha said with her hands on her hips.

"Woman, I'm not going to even give you a response. I don't know how Aijah and Anthony's situation have anything to do with our marriage, or it turning into me wanting to leave."

33

Ahlesha walked away, but not without her shouting a few more opinions about the situation. When she got to the bedroom Sean and the boys could hear the door slamming behind her.

Sean looked at the boys. "Well, I guess we're on kitchen duty."

Chapter 7

"Oh, girl, thanks for coming to help me get started on this decorating. With my assistant gone out of town, I'm beginning to feel overwhelmed." Aijah says to Ahlesha.

"Girl, no problem. You know I don't mind."

The two ladies were in the large, empty commercial space where Aijah was laying out the painter's tape to mark the areas that were to be painted. The 1,500 square foot space felt humongous as it set empty with only a few nail stations and receptionist desk. Aijah opted to do most of the decorating herself. Whenever she could she would watch all of the decorating shows on the decorating channel to get plenty of ideas for her spa.

The space had dark cherry hardwood flooring throughout. An exposed brick wall, with a large cut-out that was a separator wall from the nail salon area and the spa area. In the front part of the building there were floor-to-ceiling windows that let in much natural sunlight.

She chose a color scheme of light-tone mauve, a darkened version of lavender, with chocolate brown and creamy ivory as accent colors. The top half of the walls would display the light mauve; the color was to flow to about chair height. Then where the mauve stopped the darkened lavender would pick up and flow down to the bottom of the wall. She would have a strip of the chocolate brown color overlap where the mauve and lavender met to form a small banner. And to finish off the paint design the painter would hand-paint "Posh Studios" in cursive writing on top of the chocolate brown strip in the creamy ivory color. This design would flow throughout the entire wall spaces in the spa.

"Girl, I really love this color scheme you picked out. It's so peaceful. I think the people will really love it when it's all set." Ahlesha says as they put the painter's tape on the last wall in the spa.

"Yes, I really do hope that they love it. I'm putting my all into this dream. Girl I'm dipping deep into my savings to pull this salon off. I just hope I'm able to get some of my money back." Aijah says as she looks around the shop at the progress she and Ahlesha accomplished.

"Don't worry, you will. But I have a question. Seeing that you're still doing a lot of consulting work when will you have the time to manage this place?"

Ahlesha asking her that question made for a great way for Aijah to ask her for a favor she'd wanted to ask since she thought about opening the salon.

"Wellllll..." Aijah sang as she smiled at Ahlesha. "I was thinking. Aren't you bored at home? Haven't you been a stay-at-home mom for long enough? You went and got that fancy business degree. Why don't you put it to use and be my business manager?"

Ahlesha chuckled. "I knew you were going to ask me that when you put that silly little smirk on your face. Girl, I don't know, I have to ask my husband."

"I could smack you. You don't have to ask Sean nothing. He's probably tired of you, you're probably getting on his nerves. I'm sure he'd be happy to see you go back to work and bring some income in the house."

"What?! Sean, get tired of me? No way." They both laughed. "Girl, of course I would. With the way Sean and I have been arguing lately I definitely need to find me something to get into."

"What do you two have to argue about? He's a good man, you're a good woman. What's the problem?" Aijah asked very concerned.

"Girl, ever heard the saying don't judge a book by its cover? When a marriage looks good on the outside, you never know the cracks that are hiding behind closed doors." Ahlesha sighed.

Aijah came from the other side of the room over to where Ahlesha was standing. "What's up?" She said staring into Ahlesha's eyes.

"Lately we've just been arguing about everything. I know it's nothing but the devil, but, my God, it just seems like we're just always arguing. It all started when he got the big promotion at the bank, this new job as CFO is requiring a lot of his time. He's never home and we're not as intimate as we've been in the past."

Aijah looked on in shook. "Are you guys still having sex?"

"Yes, but not often. It just seems like we're losing our spark or something. It just came out of nowhere. This uncertainty in our marriage is just bringing up old memories." Ahlesha clears her throat. "And if I'm being honest it making me quite insecure."

"Girl, you don't have anything to worry about. Sean just has a lot going on right now. I'd rather be going through what you're going through then be in my situation any day." Aijah says comfortingly.

"Speaking of you and Anthony, that's another thing we've been arguing over a lot, too."

"Ahlesha, girl don't bring our situation into y'all's marriage. This is between me and Anthony."

"Girl, I know. But I can't help it. I'm mad at Anthony for how he's just being so foolish. How could he just leave y'all like that? And then whenever I speak to Sean about it, it's like he's on Anthony's side."

"Ahlesha, I don't think he's taking his side, but they are close friends. Maybe he understands coming from a man's perspective."

"How can you be so calm about this?"

Aijah smiles awkwardly. "Girl, nothing but God. I've learned that being optimistic ain't nothing but having faith. The Bible said to look to Jesus who is the author and finisher of our faith. I keep my mind on God in order to stop from going crazy and breaking down."

"Girl, you've always been strong. I wish God would have blessed me with half the strength he gave you."

"Ahlesha, you're strong. You've endured a lot of things, especially with Lenox. With all that you've been through and managed to come out with a man like Sean, shows you have a lot of strength."

"Yeah, I hear you. But what are you going to do if he doesn't come back home?"

Aijah purses her lips and rolls her eyes. "Girl, I'm going to move on with my life – me and my son. One monkey don't stop a show, and I'm not the first woman whose husband left her."

Ahlesha laughs. "You sound so cold. Like there's no love left in your heart."

"No. I sound like a woman who has given the situation over to God. I pray every night for Anthony. I cry sometimes, but I leave all of that at the altar. I have a lot of other things going on in my world. God is beginning to open a lot of doors up for me. If I allowed this one tragedy in my life to overtake me, I'd be no good for kingdom work."

Ahlesha smiled. "I admire you so much. You spoke that like a mighty woman of God."

"Everything is about kingdom work and the Lord being pleased with my life. With the people I've been in contact with ever since the shop was on BET, when some of them find out I'm saved and that door opens up for me to minister to them...I just get a rush." Aijah begin to get excited.

"I feel the Holy Spirit come over me and we get to talking about salvation, and God's grace and mercy. Girl you wouldn't believe me if I told you some of the celebrities I had crying on my shoulder. I stay strong because I have a charge to keep and a God to glorify."

Ahlesha began to jump up and down. "Girl, stop! You 'bout to make me shout. I can just feel and imagine you ministering to people."

"Yes, it's so amazing. I never imagined this ever happening to me. I started out as a nail tech following behind Lenox when he opened up his shop, and look at me now. I'm standing in my own spa. Hallelujah!!"

They both started praising the Lord right then and there in the shop. They were so loud that they caught the attention of passerbys. They didn't care, they were giving glory to their God.

After shouting for another few minutes Aijah felt full of faith. So much in that she thought about the state of her marriage, and that God was powerful enough God to put her marriage back together.

Aijah turned to Ahlesha. "You know what I'm thinking about?"

"What?" Ahlesha looked on with glistening eyes.

"I'm thinking of calling Anthony and telling him to come back home."

"Well ain't nothing wrong with that. You think he will?"

"I don't know. We haven't been arguing as much when we see each other anymore. But besides that, I really, really miss him. Whenever we're around each other I just still sense a connection. I'm not sure if I'm just in denial that our marriage is over, but I think there is still something there."

"Well the Word did say that two will become one. So I can understand that connection that you may be feeling and longing for."

"Yes, I'm longing for my friend to come back home. I still love him just as much as I did when we first got married. He may not can tell because I'm so mean to him when he comes around, but that just because I'm hurt about the situation. But when he leaves, oh how I wish that he would have stayed."

"Well, girl, a closed mouth definitely doesn't get fed. So gone ahead and call your man and tell him to come back home."

"I most definitely will. You're going to have to be free to baby sit for me. I'm going to invite him home for dinner and seduce him. It's been long enough I'm sure he won't be able to resist me."

They both giggle like school girls, Aijah even blushes a little as she thinks about the possible reunion of her and Anthony.

Chapter 8

The following weekend after Ahlesha and Aijah were at the new spa, Aijah finally had enough courage to call Anthony over. She'd taken baby Jason over to Ahlesha's house for the weekend. She went back to her home to turn it into a lover's den.

She went out and purchased some white and red roses and plucked the petals off and scattered them in the bedroom and around the dinner table. She cooked a dinner of filet mignon, roasted, baby red potatoes, fried green tomatoes, and steamed broccoli. All of these foods were Anthony's favorite foods. She even bought some sparkling juice to go along with their dinner to make it more formal. She set the table with some of her best China, pulled out their crystal wedding flutes, and lit some romantic candles.

It took some convincing to get Anthony to agree to come over. She told him that she wanted to talk, but he said that they could talk over the phone. She insisted that she preferred to speak in person and that she'll make it worth his while. Anthony conceded and agreed to meet her at the house at 7:00pm.

6:45 rolled around and Aijah could feel the butterflies in her stomach as she was nervous to see her husband in that way after such a long period of time. The reality of the nearly year-long separation began to feel overwhelming to her as she thought upon it.

She sat at the elegantly set dinner table in a sexy black, causal knee-length dress. She wore some cute Chanel sandals, as she didn't want to look like she was trying too hard with her attire.

As the clocked rolled around to 6:52 she saw two headlights pull into the driveway. The fifty butterflies she felt in her belly quickly turned into five-hundred. She wasn't sure if she should meet him at the door or if she should wait for him to ring the bell.

Anthony ended up making the decision for her – he used his key to let himself in.

Aijah shook her head and stood up to meet him as he came around the corner to the dining room. "I thought I told you to give me my key back?" She asked in a seductive way.

Anthony was surprised at the scene that he saw that was laid out for him. "I thought you said that you wanted to talk?" He said.

"I do. But is it anything wrong with *talking* over dinner?" Aijah smiled.

Now Anthony was shaking his head. "Girl, you know you're crazy. You were just going off on me a couple of days ago, now you're cooking me dinner?"

"You're talking about the discussion we were having? I wasn't going off, it was just a very exciting conversation."

"Whatever you say. So what's for dinner?" Anthony says as he sits down at the table.

"Oh nothing but your favorites. Filet mignon, broccoli, baby red potatoes, and fried green tomatoes."

"Aww man, you must have something very important you want to discuss. You didn't hold anything back, huh?"

"Let's just eat and we'll talk later."

Aijah proceeded to the kitchen and fixed both of their plates. She delivered them into the dining room. As she was setting Anthony's plate in front of him she made sure that she brushed her body softly up against the right side of his body. She was wearing her favorite perfume, Chanel No. 5 and the scent intoxicated Anthony.

She went to her side of the table and sat her plate down and sat in the chair. They both ate in silence for about seven minutes. Aijah takes a few sips of the sparkling juice and stared at Anthony.

He was looking down the entire time never looking up once. The silence was too intense for Aijah. She was silently going over in her head how she was going to start the conversation she lured him over for.

Before she knew it, she blurted out, "I want you to come back home."

45

Anthony stopped mid-way from bringing his fork, with his piece of filet mignon on it, to his mouth. He looks up connecting his eyes to Aijah's instantly. "What?!"

Aijah cleared her throat. "I want you to come home. I miss you."

Anthony didn't say a word, he continued to stare at Aijah as if she was speaking in a foreign language.

Aijah, now feeling awkward spoke. "Are you going to say something? This is what I called you over here for."

"I don't know what to say, Aijah."

"Well I can help you with that answer. Say, yes." She lifts up from her chair. "Say yes you'll come home." Aijah pleads.

Aijah walks over to Anthony's seat and grabs his hand. She pulls him out of his seat and walks him to the bedroom. Aijah took Anthony's silence as his obliging to her request.

When they get to the room he surveys it as he embraces the seductive smell of the cashmere wood and vanilla scented candles that were burning. Aijah had about six candles burning in the room, which caused shadows of the lit wicks to sensually dance against the walls. The low light also illuminated the red and white rose petals, whose fragrant aroma mixed with the scent of the candles.

Aijah pushed Anthony on the bed, climbed on top of him and began kissing him. She forgot what it felt like to kiss his lips after so long. She melted in the warmth of his lips and arms as he appeared to be succumbing to Aijah's advances.

They passionately kissed until Anthony abruptly stopped. He carefully moved Aijah to side and stood up.

"Aijah, this is not a good idea. It would be stupid of us to go this way."

Aijah felt crushed, but she thought that Anthony was just nervous after not being together for so long.

"You don't have to be nervous, baby. We have the whole weekend to work out our nerves. Just relax and let's enjoy one another." She got up off the bed and tried to kiss him again. But Anthony resisted and pushed her backwards.

"No, Aijah. We can't do this. This was a bad idea."

Anthony pulled his keys from his pockets and swiftly ran out of the room, then out of the front door.

Aijah was hurt. She didn't expect for the scene to end in that way. She thought they would be cuddling in each other's arms telling each other how much they've missed each other. But instead she was left standing in the middle of a romantic setting crying all of her hurt and pain from that moment.

"God what is going on?" She screamed from the top of her lungs. She clinched her chest and fell to the floor. The pain she felt was unexplainable. It opened the wound in her heart from when Anthony left the day after their fourth-year anniversary.

"Oh, God, it hurts so bad. Cover me, cover me dear Lord. This hurts so bad. Hold my hand and comfort me." Aijah pleaded out to the Lord as she looked to him to stop her from having a nervous breakdown for the cold-hearted hurt she felt.

For a second Aijah was depressed. She went into the living room, blew out the candles, then back to the bedroom and blew out those candles. She pulled her satin covers back from the bed, climbed in and pulled the covers over her head. She slept with a broken heart that evening.

The next day she woke up with heavy heart. She knew that Sunday morning she was going to need a push from the Lord to get her through. She got up out of the bed and walked into the kitchen to find the food still sitting out from the evening before.

She wrapped everything up and placed them in containers and put them in the refrigerator. After cleaning up the kitchen and dining area she took a shower. As she came out from the bathroom draped in her towel, she canvassed her closet to see what she was putting on. She spotted her black suit and felt that it was appropriate to match the dark mood she was in.

She decided not to wear much makeup because every time she thought about what happened the night before she would cry a little. Even as she got in the car, the song playing on the radio made her have a small breakdown in the car. "Take me to the king. I don't have much to bring. My heart is torn to pieces, here's my offering." The song lyrics powerfully sung by Tamela Mann.

She grabbed her large, dark tinted glasses that she liked to wear in the car. She especially liked these glasses because she would be able to still shed her tears privately behind her shades. Other drivers that may have caught a glimpse of her wouldn't be able to tell that she was crying in her car.

As she was driving to church she continued to pray and ask the Lord to please give her a word of comfort to help lift her spirits.

When she arrives at Temple of Emmanuel she comes in when the choir is on their second selection. She spots Sean and Ahlesha sitting with their two boys, and little Jason. Ahlesha had saved a seat for her; Aijah came in and softly took her seat.

Walking in to the church, no one would have ever known that she cried the entire twenty-minute drive it took her from her home to the church. When she pulled in the parking lot she used her compressed powder and slightly touched up the areas that showed tear marks. She also dropped in her eye drops to clear the redness that resulted from her crying.

As normal, Aijah got in the praises and joined in with the congregation. The churches motto is "leave your problems at the door, and pick up the praises." And that is exactly what she did.

After the choir's selection, on cue Pastor Richards came down and greeted the congregation with praise. He began his sermon and Aijah was intently listening to every word he spoke. Aijah knew that the Word of God came with strength and hope, and she definitely wanted to take some of it home with her.

Pastor Richards had somewhat of an unexpected sermon on that day. He spoke about moving on. The sermon came from the very familiar scripture in Philippians, chapter three. Apostle Paul famously tells the saints to press toward the prize of the high calling of God.

"My people we have to move on in life. The devil comes to beat us down, get us up against a wall, troubles us on every side. But we have to remember that we have a great destiny ahead of us that we can't afford to lose ground." Pastor Richards thundered on in his sermon.

"Press, my people, PRESS!!" He screamed. "All things work together for the good of them that love God. Don't look at your circumstances, but look to Jesus."

When Pastor Richards said that he reminded Aijah of her fight, and how she has been able to sustain her strength through the entire separation. She dusted the gloom and doom off of her shoulders and felt renewed. She didn't let the rejection of Anthony control her feelings any longer. She made up in her mind that very second that she needed to move on. She was moving on with or without Anthony.

Chapter 9

It had been a couple of days since Aijah seen Anthony after he rejected her. They hadn't exchanged texts or phone calls during the time. Aijah could have cared less; she'd given the situation to God and kept it moving.

Anthony was coming to pick up Jason for a couple of days, Aijah was in the middle of preparing his overnight bag when she heard the doorbell ring. *Dang, he's early.* She thought.

She gets up from the floor in Jason's room where she was sitting preparing his clothes. She rushes to the front door.

"Hey." She says as she opens the door to let Anthony in.

"Hey." Jason responds.

He steps back and doesn't come in the door. Aijah looks puzzled, he normally would come in and sit in the living room while she gets Jason ready.

"What's wrong with you? Are you coming in?"

"Nah, I'll just wait outside."

Aijah slightly tilts her head. *No, this negro ain't acting like he scared to come into my house.*

"You don't want to come in?" Aijah says.

"Nah, I'll just stay out here while you get him ready?"

"Fine, stay out in the hot sun then." Aijah slams the door.

Aijah was flabbergasted at Anthony's behavior. She was also insulted that he would take the incident so far as to not want to come in her home. She purposely took her time getting Jason's bag together. Anthony ended up standing outside for about twenty minutes.

"What took you so long?" Anthony says frustrated.

Aijah bends down to Jason. "Ok, baby, give mommy a hug and kiss." Jason leans in and gives Aijah a kiss - she never responds to Anthony.

"So you're going to ignore me?"

Aijah laughs. "No one told you to stand outside."

"Whatever. You can be so childish sometimes." Anthony grabs Jason's hand, snatches Jason's overnight bag from Aijah's hand, then leads Jason to his car.

"Childish? You're the childish one. You're acting funny like you don't want to come in the house. You have the biggest ego for no reason." Aijah yells as Anthony is putting Jason in the car.

"Aijah, just shut up talking to me."

Aijah was ready to walk back into the house, but Anthony's reply infuriated her more.

"*Shut up talking to you?* Did you really just say that? What reason did I give you to say that to me? You need to

hurry up and get off my property before we have a problem."
She says while walking up to the car.

"Don't forget it's my property, too." Anthony said with
a smirk. "I can sit here in my car, on my property as long as I
like. Actually I can come back in *my* house and sit down if I
like."

"Ok, now you're playing games. Just leave. I see what
you're trying to do, you trying to push my buttons – but the
devil is a lie."

"Baby, the devil ain't got nothing to do with this."
Anthony says while leaning on his car on the driver's side
with the car door open.

Aijah decided that she was going to be the bigger
person and not add more fuel to the fire. She waved Anthony
off and went into the house.

Anthony stood for a couple more seconds as he
watched Aijah go into the house. He didn't know why he was
messing with Aijah. He knew that she kept him outside
waiting because she felt slighted that he didn't come in. He
normally is not an instigator of situations but he couldn't help
himself. Anthony finally gets in his car and drives off.

When Aijah heard Jason drive off tears came rushing
out from her eyes. She thought she had cried enough on
Sunday at church, but there was still some residual pain
from the rejection.

"Why do I still want a man that clearly wants nothing to do with me?" She screamed out into the air. "Why do I still love him?" She continued to scream and ask herself.

Aijah let many things go through her mind. She wished that she could just go out and get her another man. Yes she was saved and sanctified, but her flesh was feeling rejected. She wanted someone to show her the opposite of what Anthony had given her. She knew that the last thing she needed to think about was sex, but, oh, how she just wanted to drown her sorrows in it. She wanted to feel the arms of a man around her, she wanted some comforting.

Aijah was doing her best to lean on the Lord, and given the time that she and Anthony had been separated she was doing good. But the more the time went by, the more it became a reality to her that she and Anthony were over. As she sat at her kitchen table with tears flowing she accepted that her marriage was dead. She started to hyperventilate.

"Oh, God!" Aijah cried out. She cried even harder.

She grabbed her purse and pulled out her cellphone to text him. She was really hurt by him and just wanted to let him know – even though she knew it wouldn't make a difference to Anthony.

She began texting… "All the rules say I shouldn't give you the satisfaction of letting you know how much you've hurt me, but man, you're really breaking my heart. It hurts to lose my friend that I thought was forever. You said 'til death do us part – you lied."

Aijah hit the send button. She called her assistant and told her to cancel all of her appointments that day. After speaking with her she threw her phone down on the table. She went into her bedroom, climbed in her bed, got under the covers and went to sleep. She slept that entire day away…Anthony never replied to her text.

Chapter 10

Weeks went by after the debacle with Anthony. Aijah used the negative energy and poured it into getting her salon and spa together for the grand opening. She was so happy that her assistant, Melissa, and Ahlesha were helping her get everything in order. There was so much buzz going around town about Aijah's new salon and spa that she was forced to make it a red-carpet event.

Because of Aijah's connections at the news stations there was a ton of press representatives calling her so that they could get interviews and press passes for the grand opening. She also had A-list celebrities calling to inform her that they would be in town to celebrate her new venture. Aijah was feeling on top of the world. This was the much needed lift she needed in her spirit to help her get pass her situation with Anthony. It definitely helped her take her mind off him.

Aijah arrived at the salon and almost cried when she saw the large banner that said, "Welcome to the Grand Opening" hanging from the building's awning. The awning was bronze in color with the wording "POSH STUDIOS" in a fancy, italicized font in mauve and lavender color. The business hours were also on there in white lettering. She also noticed that the press was there earlier than expected, even though the event wasn't schedule to start for another three hours at 7:00pm.

There was a mauve carpet scrolled out, taking the place of the traditional rep carpet, and a white backdrop with the POSH STUDIO logo patterned across for everyone to take pictures in front of. After taking in the scene, Aijah drove her car around to the private parking area that she had built for her celebrity clients. She also made a private entrance as well, so that celebrities could be serviced without distraction.

She walked into the spa interrupting about a dozen interns, her new employees, her assistant, Melissa, and Ahlesha orchestrating the entire setup.

When everyone saw Aijah walk in they all yelled, "Congratulations!"

Aijah had to hold back her tears as she was in awe of everything that was transpiring. Ahlesha rushed over to her side and gave her a hug.

"So how you like?" Ahlesha said with a huge smile on her face.

"Girl, it's better than I expected. Y'all doing a great job in here." Aijah surveyed the room.

Although all of the spa's equipment was in place they really made it look nice by having high-boy tables set up sporadically throughout the spa. The tables were for the guest to place their beverages and appetizers on so they could feel relaxed and not have to hold their items all night. Aijah also thought of having some gift bags prepared for guests. She put in some travel-size lotions and oils from the company that she was using for her spa products and some fifteen-percent off coupons for customers in the bags. Aijah was also feeling very generous, in five of the bags there was a coupon for a free manicure and pedicure service and massage service. Aijah wanted to let everyone know that she was in the business of presenting quality, high-class service. She also wanted to make sure that her clients came back to help her make the money back she'd spent getting the place together.

After all of the hustle and bustle of putting everything in its place, Aijah had only an hour and a half to get her makeup done and get dressed. Her office looked like a disaster area compared to the rest of the elaborately decorated spa; thank God it was closed off and private. Her makeup artist gave her a natural look with brown and gold toned eye shadows and natural pink lips. She wore her hair in a huge, curly twist-out afro. She had custom t-shirts designed for the grand opening; they were white with the POSH STUDIOS logo on the fronts. Aijah's shirt had an extra flare added, she had "Head Diva In Charge" written on hers. She paired her top with some designer pant, leggings that were brown with an intricate pattern on them with shades of purples and pinks, and some nude, t-strap stilettos.

Aijah looked hot and felt like a superstar. When she came out of her office to give the "before the event" speech everyone's mouth dropped to the floor.

"Girl, you look the bomb!!" Ahlesha said enthusiastically.

"Thank you, thank you!!" Aijah said smiling. "I better look the bomb. I'm a celebrity stylist on the rise. I have to wow them tonight; I have to use this opportunity to gain some new clients."

Aijah spent the next fifteen minutes directing her staff and helpers on what she wanted to see go on and getting everyone hyped up for the special evening. Soon the press-photographers were entreating Aijah to come out of the shop for pre-event press photos, she also had her own photographer there to get photos.

As the time drew near guests began to show up. They were excited about the "mauve carpet" and definitely took advantage of the photo opportunity with the head diva in charge. Aijah didn't mind taking pictures with her future clients, and tried to get as many in as she could before she got pulled away when some of the bigger names arrived.

Eventually the spa was packed to capacity; everyone was hob-knobbing and enjoying themselves. Aijah, Sean, and Ahlesha were standing talking when Lenox finally arrived at the party. Aijah immediately got on guard because although it had been years since Lenox and Ahlesha were together, it was no secret to everyone that he still had feelings for her – and Sean was well aware.

"Oh, boy, here go this fool." Aijah says.

They all stand at attention as they watch Lenox come walking toward them.

"Hey, big brother!" Aijah says.

Lenox leans in and gives Aijah a big hug. "Hey, baby sis! The place looks great! I'm so proud of you." Lenox looks around and takes in the scene. "What you trying to do? Out do your big brother? You got some people in here that even I couldn't pull. I guess that's that favor you're always talking about, huh?"

"Yeah, that's that favor. You need to get on the winning side so God can sprinkle some of it on you." They both laugh.

Then Lenox's attention gets on Sean and Ahlesha. He smiles and extends his hand to Sean. "Hey how you doing, man?"

"I'm good how about you?" Sean extends his hand to connect with Lenox's and they shake.

Then Lenox looks to Ahlesha. "Heeeyyyy! How's the mother of my son doing?" He leans in and gives Ahlesha a hug.

Ahlesha hugs Lenox back. The hug lasted a little too long for Sean's liking so he cleared his throat to remind Lenox that he was still standing there. Lenox releases Ahlesha and lets out a slight chuckle.

"Hey, Lenox, how are you?" Ahlesha says.

Lenox laughed. "Look y'all we're not going to act like we don't see each other often. Let's just relax have a good time to celebrate Aijah. Everyone is looking good and I'm ready to party..." Lenox paused for a second. "I guess I won't be partying too much. I forgot you goodie-goods don't drink."

"Whatever, Lenox. You don't have to get drunk to have a good time." Aijah says as she waved him off. Aijah spotted Lisa, the lead evening news anchor from the Channel 9 news station. "Hey, I have to go say hi to Lisa. You all behave yourselves while I'm gone." She pointed her finger individually all three of them.

"Awww. Ain't nothing gon' happen. Sean got his wife on lockdown." Lenox said sarcastically.

Sean scoffed. "Baby, I'm stepping to the car I'll be back." Sean always let Lenox get to him. After four years he should be used to Lenox's tactics, but he always ended up allowing him to get under his skin.

Lenox and Ahlesha was left standing alone. After Lenox felt that the room was clear he did what he normally did whenever he got a chance to be alone with Ahlesha.

"Well you're looking fine as ever. You know you should be my wife." Lenox said as he schmoozed up to Ahlesha.

"Lenox, cut it out. Don't be disrespectful." Ahlesha said stepping back away from Lenox.

"Whatever, you know you still want me, too."

"Lenox, please. I'm happily married." Ahelsha says while putting her hand up in his face.

Lenox snaps his teeth at Ahlesha as if he was going to bite her. She quickly pulls her hands back.

"You didn't seem too happily married a few months ago."

Ahlesha eyes grew big. "Lenox!" Ahlesha softly yelled. "Now, you know I didn't have anything to do with that. That was you and your aggressive ways as usual."

"Whatever, you know you liked it." Lenox says.

"Liked what?" Aijah says as she happens to come in on their conversation.

"Nothing." Ahlesha said as she rolled her eyes at Lenox and walked away, while Lenox stood there laughing.

"What's that all about?" Aijah gives Lenox a stern look.

"Nothing. Nothing at all." Lenox didn't give Aijah an answer, but the uncomfortableness said it all. Lenox spots some people he knew and excused himself from Aijah.

"Well, well, well. We meet again. How are you, Mrs. Waters?" A deep strong voice says behind Aijah.

Aijah turns to find that it's the fine Calvin Perkins, the entertainment lawyer she met at the news station.

Aijah blushes slightly. "Hey. How are you? How'd you know about my party?" Aijah was impressed and happy to see Calvin.

"Sweetheart, it's the talk of the town. Why wouldn't I come? When I found out that it was you who was opening this spa I had to come see you."

Aijah blushed some more. She was flattered that Calvin had come to visit her and seemed to be interested in her.

"Well thanks for coming. I hope you become a frequent client. You know, this spa is not just for women?" Aijah smirked.

"Yes! I most definitely will be visiting…frequently. Can I have a tour?"

"Sure. Follow me."

As Aijah walks away Calvin grabs Aijah's hand. Him touching her caught her off guard and caused her to pull back.

"Oh, I'm sorry. Too forward?" Calvin asks.

"Yes." Aijah says.

Calvin throws his hands up as to surrender then suggests that she leads the way.

After the short tour of the spa, Aijah and Calvin find a cozy place near one of the facial stations. There is an entire party going on in honor of Aijah, yet she's engulfed in a deep, mind titillating conversation with Mr. Calvin Perkins. As he's talking to her she can't help but let her mind drift and begin to stop listening to the words he's saying, but study every curve of his light-skinned face. She noticed his full beard and her eyes wrapped around every curve of the beard. She even notices the sporadic gray hairs that were trying to peak out through the black beard. Then she looks at his long eyelashes that complimented his grayish-brown eyes. She also admired his light brown freckles and mole that was cutely place on the side of his right nostril.

As she was slowly imagining herself caressing his face with her hands a familiar voice caught her attention.

"To whom do I have the pleasure of meeting that has my wife so engaged in conversation?"

Aijah smacked her lips as if she was irritated. She turned and locked eyes immediately with Anthony. He actually looked handsome wearing a white, fitted t-shirt, with his white, washed jeans, and black slim fit vest. And as usual his deep, jet black waves in his hair shined, complimenting his caramel complexion.

Calvin stood up straight from leaning against the wall they were standing near. He extended his hands to Anthony; Anthony shook his hand. They exchanged hellos.

Calvin was slightly embarrassed. Here he was cozying up to a woman that he didn't know was married. Anthony rarely came up to the shop when she worked for Lenox, and any events that Aijah went to she was usually alone or Ahlesha accompanied her. So it was really shocking to Calvin to find out that she was married because he never seen her with a guy friend.

"Well I'll just excuse myself. Nice meeting you." Calvin said to Anthony.

"What are you doing here?" Aijah says.

"Oh...I wasn't invited?" Anthony says sarcastically.

"No. I didn't say that. I'm just surprised you came. I didn't even know that you knew about the grand opening."

Anthony smirked. "I know we're separated but I'm not that far removed from your life that I wouldn't know that you were having a grand opening."

Aijah shrugs her shoulder. "Well did you take a look around? Do you like it?"

"Yeah, you did a good job. You were always talented. I had no doubt in my mind that the salon would be anything less than stellar."

Aijah allowed herself to be slightly flattered. She still had a trivial grudge against Anthony for the way he acted that day at the house.

For the rest of the night Aijah couldn't shake Anthony from her side. Meanwhile Calvin continued to stick around.

66

Calvin and Aijah managed to steal looks of each other with the occasional eye contact whenever they could.

Lenox eventually left the grand opening after getting on Sean and Ahlesha's nerves the entire time he was present.

Chapter 11

It had been a good month since the official opening of POSH STUDIOS. The press from the grand opening generated a lot of attention for Aijah and the spa. She received the main story of the around town section of all the local newspapers. Local blogs of the area were singing her high praise. The celebrities that showed up to the event posted their selfies and pictures from the event. Aijah was instantly a hot commodity among Chicago urban nail salons and spas.

In one day the salon's appointments were booked with a two week waiting list. For a new salon that was actually a good thing and meant that she definitely was in demand. Even her celebrity clients referred some of their celebrity friends, making Aijah an official celebrity stylist and nail technician.

After a busy Tuesday night at the spa, Aijah and Ahlesha were closing up. Ahlesha was counting down the registers and booking all the sales from the day, and Aijah was reviewing the calendar of appointments and prepping the spa for the next day's business.

"We had a good day today, for a Tuesday." Ahlesha said.

"Really? What does a 'good day' look like?" Aijah responds back as she's tidying up the waiting area.

"We made $10,000 today."

Aijah stopped dead in her tracks. "What? $10,000? Are you sure?? Did you count the sales right?"

Ahlesha laughed. "Yes, Aijah! I do have a MBA. I think I know how to count."

"No, I'm not trying to be smart. But we've never made that much in one day before."

"Yes, ma'am. We made ten grand today. If we stay on this track we're definitely going to have a good first year." Ahlesha said shaking her head up and down.

"Wow!" Is all Aijah could say.

"You would think that you were the one that had the MBA. You're business plan was smart, I don't think I would have ever thought of that." Alesha said to Aijah.

When designing her spa, Aijah took her queue from the Asian salon owners. They maximize their money making potential by having an excess of available technicians. But Aijah didn't want to cheapen the experience for her clients, She had custom booths made that allowed clients privacy when getting their nails done. She also came up with a great floor plan that allowed for the maximum amount of technicians.

She also ensured that she stepped up her game in terms of the services that she offered. She wanted to make sure that she was a step ahead of all other spas out there so that her boutique pricing was justified.

Just as Aijah and Ahlesha were getting ready to close up shop the spa's phone ranged. Both ladies looked at each other wondering who could be calling as such an hour.

"I'll get it." Aijah said to Ahlesha. "POSH STUDIOS, how can I help you?"

"May I speak to Mrs. Waters?" The deep voice asked.

"This is she. May I ask whose calling?" Aijah asked hesitantly.

"It's Calvin."

Aijah melted. She had been listening to his voice by memory ever since the day of the grand opening. Although she was still married and hoped of a reconciliation, Aijah couldn't help but to be attracted to the attention she received from Calvin.

"Hey Calvin, how are you? Long time no hear from."

While Aijah is blushing from the phone call, Ahlesha is looking on wondering who she is speaking to.

"Aww yeah I know. But your husband scared me off." He says jokingly. "Why didn't you tell me that you were married?"

"Well our conversation never entered into the realm for me to have to tell you that I was married."

"Who is that?" Ahlesha mouths to Aijah as she looks upon her smiling from ear to ear.

"I guess you have a point. I hope I didn't cause any friction. Did I?" Calvin replies.

Aijah puts her hand over the phone receiver so that Calvin couldn't hear her. "It's Calvin Perkins." Aijah says to Ahlesha.

"Oooooo." Ahlesha responds.

"No. You didn't. We're good." Aijah says to Calvin as she returns back to the conversation.

Aijah didn't care to enlighten him on her and Anthony's separation, plus Ahlesha was distracting her by being nosy. Although she was flattered by Calvin's attention she still loved her husband and had hope that one day they would reconcile. Ahlesha waves to Aijah to signal to her that she was leaving and whispered to her to make sure she locks up and not to stay too late. Aijah waves back and gives her the thumbs up to acknowledge she heard her.

"Well your husband is a lucky man to have such a beautiful woman by his side." Calvin says.

Aijah rolled her eyes. *Yeah, wished he knew that.* Aijah thought. "Well yeah. So what brings you to call?" Aijah wanted to change the subject.

"Well I was wondering if you were interested in taking on another consulting project?"

"Wow. Well my plate is pretty full here at the spa and I'm currently consulting on three major projects right now."

71

"Come on you don't want to miss out on this one. Besides I kind of put my foot in my mouth by telling the person that wants you for the project that I knew you well. So I need you to help me." Calvin laughs.

"Oh really?! So you need me, huh? What's in it for me if I help you?"

"I can reward you to a five-star dinner at *Capital Grille* downtown. How's that?"

"I've never been there before. So it better be good."

"Yeah it's fantastic. You won't be disappointed." Calvin says with excitement in his voice.

"But wait a minute. I still don't know what this new project is."

"Well do you know who Ronda Shines is? The producer and creator of shows like *Interns and Residents* and *Slander*?"

Aijah puts her hands over her mouth to contain her excitement. "Yes, of course I know who she is." She says as she released her hand.

"Good. She's producing a new show called, *Working Girls* and she needs a costume consultant."

"*Working Girls*? Is the show about prostitutes?"

Calvin laughs out loud. "No. From what I read it's about the lives of three high-profile business executive bachelorettes looking for love."

"Oh, ok - sounds interesting. How did you get hooked up with the show?"

"Well they're filming here in Chicago and she wanted to hire a local entertainment lawyer. One of our mutual friends introduced us and she hired me."

"Oh wow! I guess it does pay to know people, huh?"

"Yeah, I guess it does. Anyway, in one of our meetings she was saying that she wanted to hire a stylist who knew Chicago's style so that the show could be authentic. I mentioned your name and she went crazy…in a good way."

"Wow. I didn't know my name stretched that far."

"Yeah, I guess God got plans for you." Calvin says.

"So it seems…" Aijah says.

Calvin continued to tell Aijah about the show and when it was scheduled to start filming. They confirmed a time when Aijah would be able to meet with Ronda and they ended their phone call. Aijah made sure that Calvin had her cell number and the number to her assistant so that he could contact her more conveniently.

Aijah couldn't believe the favor that she was seeing on her life. Through the entire ordeal with Anthony she was determined to remain faithful to God. She maintained a strong spiritual life because she knew that God was the only source that could uphold her. She never missed a prayer meeting, shut-in, Bible study or Sunday service. She believed that God was now openly rewarding her for keeping the faith and not allowing her trials and tribulation to steer her away from His presence.

She spent the next ten minutes in the shop giving praises to God for the potential open door and prayed that she has a successful meeting with Ms. Shines. Aijah was very appreciative for all the blessings that were happening to her.

Chapter 12

"So what time are you coming to pick up the boys?" Ahlesha asked Lenox over the phone.

Although Sean, Jr. wasn't Lenox's biological son, he never thought it was fair to pick up Maurice and not allow his brother to come with him. Lenox may have had many bad qualities, but one thing about him was true, he had a heart for children. Ahlesha and Sean, Sr. knew that the boys were safe when they were with him.

"I'll be there around noon. Will your husband be there?" Lenox asked.

"Yes, he will. You know you need to stop this. What you do at times is very inappropriate and makes me uncomfortable." Ahlesha says irritated.

"Well you need to stop sending mixed messages then."

"What mixed messages do I send you? Please, do tell." Ahlesha yelled over the phone.

"The last time we had a chance to be really alone you were all over me. It seemed like you enjoyed it, too."

Ahlesha laughed. "Lenox, you're delusional. First of all, you kissed me. The kissed maybe lasted five seconds, and then I immediately put you out."

"Whatever, you may have pushed me back, but it felt like it was more to it to me."

One evening a few months back Sean was out with the boys having father and sons day. Lenox stopped by the house to drop off some clothing that he'd purchase for the boys. When Lenox realized that Ahlesha was home alone he decided to make himself at home.

Ahlesha was used to Lenox's advances toward her, but she was completely caught off guard this particular day. While Ahlesha was walking Lenox back to the front door to let him out, Lenox pulled her to him and started kissing her. Ahlesha was shocked for a moment but her reflexes caused her to push back and she kicked Lenox out.

"Lenox, why don't you settle down with Tameka and be happy. Why are you still chasing after me?"

"Because you're supposed to be my wife. Sean was never supposed to have you."

"Lenox, let it go. And besides I don't think it's me that you want, it's the chase that has you attracted. You're not used to getting told no and it's killing you."

"I should have held on longer to you. I gave up too easily. All because I was afraid of waiting..."

Ahlesha cut Lenox off before he could finish his sentence. "Lenox, stop the madness. You know that you weren't going to wait for me. Besides the man I have is exactly what I want and who I want. Nothing's more sexier than a man that loves God, who is serving God with his whole heart, and is faithful to his wife."

Lenox laughs out loud. "Ha!!! Then why do you seem so bored."

Ahlesha didn't have a comeback statement. "Good bye, Lenox. See you at 1:00." That was all she could manage to say as she hung up the phone.

Ahlesha knew that Lenox had a point. She was indeed bored. Sean was saved and sanctified. Although Ahlesha served the Lord, too, she felt like she was missing some excitement in her marriage. It seemed like Sean didn't like to do anything outside of the church. Everything was "God, God, God" and sometimes she wanted things to be just about them two enjoying one another.

When she was with Lenox they did many adventurous and exciting things. They always took trips and explored new things. Sean was the complete opposite. He was a homebody and didn't care to do the fun things that Ahlesha desired. Lack of resources wasn't the problem because Sean's income was in the mid-six-figures, he was just a bump on a log…at least compared to Ahlesha.

****

"Whew, thank you Jesus!" Ahlesha says as she closed to door after Lenox left the house.

She managed to get him in and out of her house without incident. Sean had stepped out quickly to run an errand before Lenox arrived to pick up the boys.

Soon after, Ahlesha realized that she would be home alone with her husband so she decided to make an evening out of it. She called this new jazz restaurant, *Simone, Fitzgerald, Holiday & Co.*, that recently opened up in Chicago to make reservations. The reviews said that the food was superb and the music was great. The restaurant had a house band that played live instrumental music on Tuesdays, Wednesdays, and Thursdays. Then on Fridays and Saturdays they would have guest musicians with their bands come in and perform live. The restaurant was very unique, as they not only catered to traditional jazz music, but those of modern day and gospel jazz artists, as well.

Ahlesha felt that it would be a great night for a date night with her husband, and she was going to take matters into her own hands to spice up their marriage life.

As she sat home waiting for Sean to get back home from running his errand she went up to their bedroom to see what sexy dress she was going to wear for the evening. She also picked out his outfit as well.

After gathering their attire for the evening she grabbed her cellphone to text Sean.

"Hey bae, it's date night tonight. We're going out to this new restaurant, our reservation is for 8:00pm so don't get home too late."

After about five minutes Sean replied back. "Ok."

Ahlesha was excited with anticipation of the evening. She knew that if the night was left up to Sean they probably would have ended up staying in the house that night.

After a few hours Sean came home, he notices that Ahlesha was in the shower when he walks into their bedroom. He also notices that Ahlesha had already picked out his clothing: a navy blue casual suit, with a crisp aqua blue shirt that was on the darker side of aqua. She matched his outfit with a monochromatic blue colored, long-sleeved, knee-length form-fitting dress.

After looking at the dress he yelled out to Ahlesha while she was in the shower. "Hey, baby?"

"Yeah!" Ahlesha yelled back.

"Are we going to dinner with anyone or are we going by ourselves?"

"We're going by ourselves. This is our date night. Why do you ask?" She yells.

"Just wondering…"

Shortly thereafter the shower goes off and Ahlesha appears before Sean wearing just her soft, white bath towel with her long hair in rollers.

"Hey, baby." Ahlesha says as she walks over to him and gives him a passionate kiss.

"Hey, baby. What's up?" Sean smiled. He enjoyed the kiss and was wondering what had gotten into his wife. "You feeling a little excitable, huh?"

"Maybe. But can't a woman just be happy to see her husband? I'm excited to be with you tonight, that's all."

"Ok. Sounds good to me. So where are we going tonight?" Sean asks as he disrobed to get ready to get in the shower.

"It's a surprise. You'll find out when we get there. I don't want you to ruin the surprise by turning your nose up when I tell you where we're going."

Sean frowned slightly. "I don't do that."

"Honey, yes you do. Sometimes you can be a little closed minded."

"Whatever, babe." He says as he walked toward the bathroom.

Sean took his shower and then came back into the room. When he saw his wife in her sexy blue dress he wanted to rip her clothes off right then and there, but decided to wait until the end of the evening to take advantage of his her.

They both were dressed and looking high fashion, ready for the night out on the town. They got into their luxury car and proceeded to get their evening started. Ahlesha was very happy to be out with her man. She couldn't keep her eyes off of Sean that night, nor could she keep her hands off of him. She was starting the four-play now because she wanted the night to end with an explosion...a very, very good one.

The mood was very high energy when they got to *Simone, Fitzgerald, Holiday & Co.* There was a jazz band playing and a sultry jazz singer harmonically vocalizing to the melody. Her voice was soft and deep and it danced with the music as the patrons tentatively listened as they enjoyed their dinners.

As the hostess showed Sean and Ahlesha to their seats, they both looked around the club and soaked up the ambience. The club was set up like a traditional 1920's jazz club. The club had a large stage with a backdrop of soft, velvety cream and dark red colored drapes. There was a white, baby Grand piano with the piano player jamming on the keys. The band was also sufficiently equipped with a guitar, trumpet, saxophone, trombone player, as well as a bass player and drummer.

The club seating was setup in stadium style, rectangular booth seating that was in a cream and black marble colored setting; some with tables for those that were dinning and some with cocktail tables for those that just came for drinks and music. The club had a concrete floor with an iridescent paint overlay, with a hardwood dancing floor set right before the stage for the patrons that wanted to dance.

As they both looked around while they nestled at their table Ahlesha caught a glimpse of Sean's expression as he analyzed the club.

Ahlesha chuckled. "What's wrong?"

"Nothing's wrong just looking around."

"You don't like it?" Ahlesha asks.

Sean nodded his head yes and continued to look around. "No, it's cool. Just something I wasn't expecting that's all."

"Yeah, I bet you thought we were going to some stuffy restaurant didn't you?"

"We don't go to stuffy restaurants, they're just not this noisy, that's all."

"Look, I just wanted to do something different. Have a little fun."

Sean lifted one eyebrow. "We have fun."

"Ha! I don't know what fun you think it is to stay in the house all the time. But yeah, we have fun…sometimes."
Sean didn't reply.

Ahlesha bopped her head to the music as they waited for their food to arrive at their tables. Sean let loose just slightly, as he displayed it with the tapping of his fingers on the dining table. Soon after their waitress arrives with their food - Ahlesha ordered a blackened salmon and lobster dish, with a side of roasted potatoes and asparagus. Sean ordered a porter house steak with truffles, with a twice-baked potato and roasted corn.

They enjoyed their food and their non-alcoholic mocktails that their hostess has specially prepared for them once she discovered that they didn't drink alcohol. The two got closer together in their booth and began to snuggle with one another. As the passion grew greater Sean was eager to leave the restaurant to take his wife home and make love to her. They had an eventful ride home and ended the evening in a blissful state.

Ahlesha really enjoyed herself with her husband that night, and was glad that she took charge of their normally boring marriage.

Chapter 13

"So how was your date this weekend?" Aijah asks Ahlesha as they sit in the spa during some down time.

"Girl, it was great!" Ahlesha says ecstatically. "We had a loving evening. I really enjoyed my husband that night."

"That is good. I'm happy for you all." Aijah smiles.

"Yes, I told Sean we have to do more things like that to keep the spark alive in our marriage. You know Sean can be a little boring at times."

Both ladies laugh as Aijah didn't want to openly agree, but it was no secret that Sean was the party pooper out of the bunch.

Aijah, however, quickly changed gears as it was something she wanted to ask Ahlesha.

"Hey, Ahlesha?" Aijah asks.

"Yeah..." Ahlesha replied as she was busying herself with the appointment book.

"Do you and Lenox got something going on?"

Ahlesha stopped in her movement as she was turning the page in the appointment book. She quickly turned toward Aijah visibly shocked. "Oh, my God, Aijah! Why would you ask me that?"

"Look, I noticed that Lenox was a little too close for comfort at the grand opening. I noticed it but I was a little bit too preoccupied with the whole opening of a spa and all to say anything to you about it. It recently popped back into my mind, and inquiring minds want to know."

Ahlesha just stared at Aijah, she was debating within herself if she was going to share her secret.

Aijah continued to stare at a blank-faced Ahlesha. "Well??" Aijah says.

Ahlesha sighed. "A while back we kissed."

"What?!" Aijah interrupted before Ahlesha could get the rest of her wording out.

Ahlesha put her hands up to slow Aijah's jumping to conclusions down. "He actually kissed me, but I shut him down. You know Lenox don't take no for an answer. For some strange reason he felt that I was giving him some kind of vibe that I wanted him."

"Oh really?" Aijah says as she places her hands on her hips.

"Yes, girl, really. I don't know what to do about Lenox."

"But what about Tameka? Isn't he with her?"

"Yeah, *he's with her*. But that really doesn't mean anything. I feel sorry for her because she's just me a few years ago. Lenox is only concerned with fulfilling his wants and desires. I don't think he can truly love anyone."

"Well, you better make sure you get that in order. If I felt that something could be going, I'm sure Sean felt it, too."

Ahlesha eyes bucked out at Aijah. "You think my husband may feel that something is going on between Lenox and me?"

Aijah shrugs her shoulders. "Girl, I don't know, but you need to nip that. Jealous men are worse than women, and I don't want to have to identify your cut up body parts all over Chicago."

Both of the women laughed. Although Ahlesha knew Sean wouldn't go that far about being jealous, it bothered her to think that her husband secretly believed that her and her ex had something going on. However, now it was time for Ahlesha to switch gears.

"Speaking of married women messing around with other men...what's going on with you and mystery man?" Ahlesha said with her hands on her hips.

Aijah scrunched her eyebrows together. "Who are you talking about?"

"The light skinned mystery man that so happen to show up at the grand opening and then who mysteriously calls here a few weeks ago."

"Dang, you know you have always been nosy. How do you know the man that called here was the same guy from the grand opening?"

"Melissa told me. She's so naïve. I asked her who Calvin Perkins was and she blabbed all your business. But it was innocent. I made it seem like I was inquiring for business purposes. She told me he came to the grand opening and I put the rest together on my own. He was the only man that held your attention all evening, until Mr. Waters came in the door."

"My goodness, was it that obvious?!" Aijah screamed.

"Girl, don't hyperventilate. I thought it was a good thing if you ask me. I'm sure it gave Anthony something to think about. I know if I popped up on my spouse and someone of the opposite sex had their attention, like Mr. Perkins had yours, it would put me on alert."

"Well, nothing is going on. He's a business friend that's all. We've only had one business dinner, that's all."

"A *business dinner*? You had a business dinner with this man and didn't tell me? What was the dinner about?"

Aijah rolls her eyes. "I didn't want to jinx it so I didn't tell anyone about it."

"So, what was the dinner about?" Ahlesha says eagerly.

"He's a legal consultant for a new TV series being produced by Ronda Shines, and I met with them to possibly be the costume consultant on the project."

"And again, you didn't tell me?" Ahlesha bucked her eyes at Aijah.

"Girl, I just told you why. I didn't want to get anyone all excited for nothing. This industry can be fickle and I just wanted to wait until I knew the outcome."

"So, did you get the job?" Ahlesha asks in anticipation.

"I don't know yet. She said that she had a few other meetings with other stylist. She said that she would let me know something in a few weeks. The production doesn't start for another few months – so if I do get it, it will be a while before I find out."

"Wow, that's so good! Praise God! But I still wish you would have told me, but it's cool."

Aijah just shook her head at Ahlesha.

But Ahlesha wasn't done with the conversation. "So, back to Mr. Perkins. What's his story?"

Aijah rolled her eyes. "He's an entertainment lawyer. I'm surprise you don't remember his face. He was at a lot of the parties that we attended when I was at Lenox's shop and other industry parties."

"Girl, you know I was only there for the free food. I wouldn't remember half of the faces if I were to see them again."

"Yeah, actually I never noticed him from the parties either, but I do remember him coming to the shop every now and then."

"So how did you two become official *friends*?" Ahlesha gave a sarcastic smirk.

"He requested my styling services for an interview he had with Channel 9 evening news one day, and we sort of kept in touch from there."

"Do you like him? Ahlesha asked frankly.

"No, I do not like him." Aijah says matter-of-factly.

"Yeah right." Ahlesha says with twisted lips.

"What?! I don't. I think he's very flattering, but I still love my husband."

"I know you love your husband. But right now someone is giving you the attention you wished your husband was giving you. It's natural for you to allow those feelings to develop."

"First of all, I'm a woman of God. How could I be showing Christ, if I let the first good-looking man that comes my way steer me away. That's a foolish woman if you ask me."

Ahlesha didn't have a comeback for it she just sat and listened to Aijah vent.

"Also I still believe that there is hope for my husband and I. God joined us together, and He said what he's joined together let no man tear it apart – that includes Anthony and me."

"Yeah, you're right." Ahlesha said.

"Yeah, I may be letting Anthony be, but that doesn't mean that I'm not still praying for us. Every now and then I can admit that my faith gets a little shaky. But that's because I begin to look at things with my natural eye, but then I look to Jesus. Marriage is full of uncertainties but I have to trust that God will stay in the midst. I'm counting on God to uphold us during this trying time."

"Amen, I feel ya. I was just concerned that's all. I know you love Anthony, and I was just making sure that you weren't giving up hope."

"No, I'm not giving up. I'm just trying to allow God to be in control and me not get in the way."

"Yeah, you definitely don't want to hinder God's plan. But do you have any idea of what could be the issue?"

"I swear it seems like this just came out of nowhere. I was truly blindsided by it. You don't just wake up and decide one day that you don't want to be married anymore. Honestly, I can't put my finger on it." Aijah sighs.

"Do you think he has another woman?"

"No, my intuition doesn't tell me that there's another woman, but I could be in denial."

"Well, it has to be something pulling him away from his family. If he's not out there cheating on you then I can't phantom in my mind why he would just up and leave his family."

"Girl, the way I look at it everything will come to light. I'm not going to worry myself with it. Trying to figure things out only makes me go crazy. Like I told you before, I'm walking on water. Walking by my faith and letting God work his power."

"Well I guess there's nothing else to say to that." Ahlesha relented.

The two women go on to discuss other topics to lighten the mood. Soon clients started to pour into the spa for services, and they shelve their conversation for another time.

Chapter 14

One day while sitting alone, Aijah realizes that it's been over a year since she and Anthony had been separated. She couldn't help but wonder why Anthony hadn't filed for divorce, yet, seeing he was the one that wanted out of the relationship. She planned on speaking to him about it when he came to pick Jason up that evening.

It was really strange. Aijah nor Jason had seen Anthony for a month. Anthony calls Aijah up one morning and told her that he had to go out of town for a month for work and wouldn't give her any more information regarding it. Aijah was used to Anthony having to make sudden trips out of town for work, but he normally tells her the itinerary and where he's going – this particular time he kept everything a secret.

Of course this secrecy put Aijah on alert. Although she was trying her best not to jump to conclusions, her imagination took her to the worst case scenario. She assumed that Anthony was ditching his son to go spend time with another woman. This was the first time that Aijah allowed the thought that Anthony had a girlfriend enter into her mind.

As she thought about it she became sick to her stomach. To think that the man she was still madly in love with was spending time with another woman made her furious. Yes, it had been over a year, but in her mind they still had lines that should not have been crossed by anyone else.

Upon realizing that she was becoming steaming mad, she regained her composure to ensure she didn't go off on Anthony when he came to pick up Jason. She wanted to be able to have a civil conversation with him regarding the status of their relationship. She soon became relieved that the wait was over when she heard the doorbell ring.

Aijah chuckled to herself that Anthony still wasn't using his keys to come in seeing that he still had his keys to the house. She swiftly walked to the door and flung it open. Her facial expression was priceless as she looked upon his new appearance.

"What did you do to yourself?" Aijah said with a concerned look on her face.

"What? You don't like it?" Anthony said as he rubbed his bald head while stepping into the doorway.

Anthony normally wore a low-cut fade with goatee and mustache, but this day he showed up with a shaven head and clean face. Aijah didn't like the look at all, if she was honest he looked very bizarre with the new look.

"Jason just laid down for a nap; let's talk for a minute while he rests." Aijah is still looking at Anthony strangely.

They both walked toward the living room and sat on the couch. It took her a minute to get used to the new style he adorned, but after staring at him for a while her husband reemerged.

"Aww, there you go." Aijah said and smiled.

Anthony laughed. "What does that mean?"

"I was just trying to look at your face and find the old Anthony that I knew. You've changed so much on me in this last year that I just don't know who you are any more."

"Well people change, Aijah."

"I know people change, Anthony. But you're becoming someone that I don't know. I don't like this person."

"Aww, here we go." Anthony said as he rested his back on the back of the couch.

"You are a morally decent person. I know your faith wasn't as strong as mine, but you were a good man - a family man. How did you let the devil come in and allow you to be taken away from your family?"

"Aijah, the devil don't have anything to do with this."

"He does! I don't know what he was speaking to your mind, but I know he was speaking. He was speaking enough to tell you to leave the wife that you love and break up your child's home."

Anthony was trying his best not to allow what Aijah was saying to penetrate his thoughts. He had successfully gotten to a point where leaving his family didn't bother him anymore and he didn't want Aijah to put the guilt trip on him.

"How could you do this to Jason, forget about me." Aijah said.

"Aijah, you act like I don't love my son. I would do anything for my son. I'm always there for my son."

"Well what happen this past month, then? How could you just disappear the way you did with no explanation. What? Were you with some woman? Was she more important than you being with your son?"

"First of all Aijah, you have no idea what you're speaking on. I told you I had to take a business trip. Secondly, no woman would ever come first before my son. Don't you know me better than that?" Anthony was frustrated.

"I just told you you're becoming someone that I don't know. So why wouldn't I be forced to come up with my own conclusions? You're sure not giving me any answers to why my family isn't a family anymore."

"I told you the answer when we first separated that this isn't working anymore."

"Well if it's not working, then why haven't you filed divorce yet? What are you waiting on? You don't want me, right?" Aijah was becoming angrier.

95

"I'm waiting on you. I don't want you fighting me in court about this. When we go I want us to go together in agreement."

"Negro, you must be crazy. That makes absolutely no sense. I've never heard of a man saying that he's waiting on the wife to be ok with the divorce before he files. You say you don't want me anymore, so it shouldn't matter if *I'm ready* or not."

"It does matter if you're ready. It's going to cost more money if we don't go together. I don't want to do the back and forth."

"Well ever heard the song, *It's Cheaper to Keep Her?* You don't get the choice to make me speed this thing along. You've made your decision, you left me. Now, you do what you want to do and let me answer in my own time. You don't get to run everything."

"Don't turn into a bitter woman." Anthony said that just to get under Aijah's skin.

Aijah looked at him in disgust. "Why are you being so cold-hearted? Are you trying to make me hate you? What is going on with you?"

"Why do you still want me?" Anthony asked sincerely.

"Because I love you."

"No, I think it's because the "church" says that we shouldn't divorce."

"Well the word of God does say that he's against divorce. But that is not my main reason why I still want you, the word is maybe ten percent of why I still want to hold on to my marriage. Yes, I love God. Loving God is what helps me look over all the mess that you've caused with us over this last year. However, I want to work on this marriage because I still love you."

"But, why?" Anthony couldn't understand how Aijah could still love him after all that he'd put her through.

"Anthony, I don't know why I love you. I don't know why I desire you to still be my husband. All I know is that I do. When I spoke my vows, they weren't words just coming out of my mouth, I meant them."

Anthony didn't say a word. He just sat there. There was silence in the room until they heard Jason cry from his bedroom. Anthony was relieved that he was awake so that they could end the conversation about their marriage.

"Look, Jason just woke up. I don't want this energy to affect him. So let's just let this be." Anthony got up from off the couch and went to Jason's room.

"Daddy!!!!" Jason sang as he stood up in his toddler bed and jumped up and down, elated to see his father after such a long time.

Aijah followed behind him and gathered Jason's items together to give to Anthony. Aijah pulls Jason off the bed and bends downs to his level.

"Ok. Mommy will see you later. Give me a big kiss and a hug." Jason hugged Aijah, but it was short. He was so happy to see his father that he rushed the good-bye with Aijah to run into his father's arms.

"Hey, son! I missed you! Give me a kiss." Jason kissed his father and they both had huge smiles on their faces.

Seeing those types of moments hurt Aijah. It bothered Aijah to have to see her son and husband leave out the door to go to another home. Home was where she was. She hated that the devil came in and tore her family apart. She knew and understood that couples go through things, but she also knew that it was never God's will for a family, or marriage to be separated.

Aijah didn't know what else to do but lean on the Lord. She had sustained all this time and knew that he wasn't going to fail her now – even through this period in her marriage. She believed God was going to put it back together but didn't know how he was going to do it.

Anthony gathered Jason and he left out the door. Aijah watched from the window as Anthony put Jason in the car and then he got in the car and drove off. Aijah felt like she didn't get a chance to say all that she wanted to say concerning their marriage. She ran to her room, pulled her cellphone out of her purse and called Anthony. After a few rings Anthony finally picks up.

"Yeah, did I forget something?" Anthony asked as he picks up.

"No. I was wondering if we could maybe go to counseling."

"For what, Aijah?"

"What do you mean *for what*? I want to work on our marriage. Maybe if we go to counseling then we can get to the root problem of what's tearing apart our marriage."

"What's tearing apart our marriage is that I just don't want to be with you anymore. I don't understand why you can't move on from that. It's been a year."

Aijah was crushed, but she could only blame herself. She put herself in the line of fire for Anthony to cut her so harshly. She heard God say leave it alone, but she just had to give one more shot. Tears began to stream down her face as she hung up the phone not wanting to hear another word from Anthony. She was so vulnerable trying to plead for his love.

"God, why do I still love him? I just don't understand it. Why can't I move on? Am I in denial or are you really telling me to hold on?"

Just as quickly as Aijah had faith, doubt crept in just as fast. Just that fast Aijah lost her hope again that things could work out in her marriage. For Aijah it would have been easier for her to deal with if Anthony was blatantly cheating on her. It would have been easier if she knew that he had a girlfriend or if he was engaged in some type of inappropriate lifestyle. But to have no official closure was what was breaking her heart. As a woman she couldn't understand how a man could wake up one morning and decide that he didn't want to be with his wife anymore.

She just wanted a reason other than he didn't want to be with her any more. Anthony never expressed that she did anything in particular to contribute to the breakdown of the marriage, and on occasion he even told her that she was a great wife. She was confused, if she was such a great wife then why was he willing to give her up? Aijah really wanted closure before she could be comfortable with the way things were going.

Chapter 15

It was a slow afternoon that Monday at Posh Studios. Many of the workers were still at their stations either watching the flat screen monitors that were sporadically placed around the spa or reading newspapers or magazines. Aijah and Ahlesha were conversing, as usual, in Aijah's office.

"Girl, so what did you do after you poured your heart out to him and he had no real response?" Ahlesha asked Aijah as Aijah was explaining the last conversation between her and Anthony.

"It was really nothing I could say. But I know this has broken me down a little bit. I opened myself up and was vulnerable, once again, and he just shut me down."

"Wow. I don't even know what to say about that. This is crazy. How could such a good man, a morally decent, family man, let the devil just come in and allow him to leave his family?"

"Yeah, that's the exact question I have. He's just changing and I don't know where this change is coming from." Aijah said with a sigh.

"Well the word does say, when an unclean spirit is gone out of a man it walk about to see whom it may devour and when it can't find rest it goes back to its house with seven other spirits. Anthony just opened himself back up to the world and allowed that devil to tell him to leave his family."

As they were talking Ahlesha heard the chime go off to signal that a client had come into the shop.

"Wow, a client. Today has been so slow. Let me go out here to see who wants some services." Ahlesha said.

As she got up to look through the two-way glass mirror that Aijah had installed she stopped in her tracks.

"Oh my, God. What is he doing here?" Ahlesha said.

Aijah stood up to see who Ahlesha was speaking about.

"Oh, I'm sorry, forgot to tell you. I invited him here. Lenox entered some of his stylist and barbers in a hair show and he wants some of my techs to do the nail art."

"Oh yeah, I wished you would have told me. I could have made myself invisible while you two talk. You know he's been acting crazy lately."

Aijah has a sorry look on her face. "Yeah, I'm sorry, girl. I'll try to make it quick."

Lenox comes strutting to the back of the spa after the front receptionist tells him where to find Aijah and Ahlesha. As he walks toward the back, Lenox admires the beauty of the shop's décor.

"Aijah, man, did I tell you how proud I am of you? You really did a great job!" He yells in their direction. When he sees Ahlesha he acts out as usual.

"Aww, there go my baby girl. How my girl doing?" Lenox says loudly trying to give Ahlesha a hug.

"Lenox gone 'head on, now." She pushes him away and walk toward the front of the shop.

"You're going to stop playing hard to get." He says as he watches her walk away.

"Lenox get in here and stop acting stupid. You have to stop being so disrespectful. She's a married woman now, after five years you haven't gotten over it, yet?"

Aijah pushes Lenox into her office and closes the door. They both sit down and go over the details of what Lenox's vision is for the hair show and what Aijah is going to have her techs do with the models' nails.

After about twenty-minutes of speaking they both come out of the office and give each other hugs.

"Ok, sweetie, I'll see you in August for the show. Thanks again."

"No, problem, big bro."

As Lenox walks back toward the front he stops at the reception desk where Ahlesha was standing speaking with the receptionist.

"So, why don't you give your baby's father a hug before I leave?" Lenox says charmingly.

"Lenox, gone. You just trying to cause problems."

"I just want a hug. I promise I'll be nice."

Ahlesha stared at Lenox for a few seconds. She sighed and reluctantly spoke. "Ok, make it quick."

Lenox embraced Ahlesha with a big bear hug and pulled her close to him. As they were hugging they heard the chime of the door opening. Lenox loosened his grip as they both turned toward the door to see who was coming in.

Ahlesha's facial expression was priceless. Of all the times she decides to give into Lenox, her husband just happens to be coming through the door. Sean barely came up to the shop during his working hours. He actually was coming to have lunch with his wife, he was trying to show some spontaneity after Ahlesha expressed to him that she was getting somewhat bored in the marriage.

Lenox seeing a moment to edge on the situation just smiled and licked his lips. He added insult to injury by extending his hand to Sean to shake his hand.

"Hey, man. How you doing?" He says with a smirk on his face.

Sean furiously smacks Lenox's hand away from him. "Dude, I don't know who you think you're dealing with, but I ain't the one. I told you before don't take my humbleness as a weakness. I've been dealing with you because of Maurice, but soon you're going to feel my wrath."

Lenox's smirk quickly turned into a serious face as he stood tall with his hands crossed at his waist, ready for the confrontation.

Sean steps a few inches into Lenox's face and spoke sternly. "This is the last time I'm going to speak to you about this. This my woman, not yours. You had your chance, but you screwed it up. Step off, play your role and don't let me have to tell you about it again."

Aijah seeing the situation escalating walked swiftly to the front of the spa and got in-between the two men.

"Hey, hey." Aijah says as pushed the two men apart. Ahlesha grabbed Sean, and Aijah opened the spa's door to escort Lenox out the door.

"We'll talk again, Mr. Alexander!" Lenox says as he winked his eye.

"No, sir. Not up in here. This will not be that type of establishment." Aijah says as she forcible pushes Lenox out the door.

Sean was ready to lunge at Lenox, but Ahlesha grabbed his arm and pulled him back.

As Sean's attention got back on Ahlesha, he yelled at her. "Take your butt in the office." He then points toward the back of the spa.

Ahlesha started to say something, but then she didn't want to make more of a scene in front of the workers that had already occurred.

The two swiftly walk into the office and Sean slams the door.

"Are you crazy?" Sean yells at Ahlesha. "How could you be so disrespectful? You and him got something going on?"

Ahlesha was surprised at Sean's asking. "What? Are you serious? Are you really asking me if I'm messing with Lenox?"

"Well, he was all up in your face at the grand opening. I also been noticing some things that I haven't spoken upon – and now you hugging dude. That didn't look like an innocent hug to me."

"Whatever, Sean. If you believe that something is going on between us, then you letting the devil mess with your mind."

"Well, you've been making it very easy for me to believe him lately. You want to do all this different stuff, trying to make me do things that you and Lenox used to do. You think I didn't notice that some of these restaurants we've been going to are spots that you and Lenox used to frequent often, when you all were together?"

"What? So you mean to tell me that just because Lenox and I went to some restaurants that we can't go together. We've been married for five years; you really need to get some confidence in the woman you've married." Ahlesha yelled back at Sean.

"So if nothing's going on, then why was Lenox sitting at my house for over an hour a few months back?"

"What are you talking about, Sean?" Ahlesha was baffled at what Sean was referring to.

Ahlesha didn't know that the day that Lenox came to the house and made a pass at her, that Sean had actually came home earlier than expected. But when he saw Lenox's car outside he pulled back out of the driveway and parked down the street to see how long it was going to take Lenox to leave his house. He never told Ahlesha about the incident because he wanted to see if Ahlesha was going to mention anything to him about it, but she never did.

Sean had been acting strangely for a while and she never knew that his strangeness was because of Lenox being at his house and he not knowing exactly what was going on between him and his wife.

"Sean, I promise you nothing is going on. Can't you see that Lenox is just trying to make you jealous?"

"Ahlesha, whatever!" Sean hollered out in frustration and pushed some papers off of Aijah's desk. He opened the office door and stormed out. He swiftly walked toward the front of the spa and rushed out.

Ahlesha was crushed. She couldn't believe that Lenox had made such a big mess between her and her husband. She leaned back on the desk and started to cry.

Aijah came rushing back to the office to check up on Ahlesha.

"Girl, you ok?"

"No!" Ahlesha yelled.

Aijah started to pick up the papers that were strung across the floor. "Girl, I've never seen Sean so upset."

"Lenox really enjoys this drama. I'm so sick of him!" Ahlesha yells again.

"Yeah, you have to nip that in bud. You don't want Lenox to be the reason why your marriage is breaking down."

Suddenly, Ahlesha lifts off the desk and grabs her purse and rushed out of the office.

"Where are you going?" Aijah yells after Ahlesha.

"I'm going to handle Lenox."

"Oh my, God!" Aijah says while putting her hands on her head in disbelief of what's going on.

Ahlesha gets in her car and speeds off. Although she wasn't sure, but seeing that it was a Monday she didn't think that Lenox went to his shop because the shop was closed on Mondays. So she decided to go to his house. After the quick twenty minute drive to the South Loop, near downtown Chicago where Lenox lived, Ahlesha pulled up to Lenox's residential building. She got out the car and handed the keys to the valet. The valet knew who she was from the previous years when Ahlesha and Lenox shared the condo in the building and her frequent trips of dropping the kids off.

"Hey, Joe! Is Mr. Jaymes home?" Joe was the head security officer of the building. He knew Ahlesha very well.

"Yes, Mrs. Ahlesha he's home. He actually just got here a few minutes ago."

"Ok, thanks." Ahlesha storms toward the open elevator car that was conveniently waiting on her. She presses the button for floor number eight. She folded her arms and tapped her foot as she waited for the car to reach his floor.

When the elevator reached its destination she hurried out and practically ran towards Lenox's door. When she arrived she banged on the door, similar to a police officer knocking on the door.

It took Lenox only a few seconds to get to the door because he was concerned at who could be knocking on his door so violently. He gets to the door and opens it up. When he sees it's Ahlesha he smiles.

"Hey, baby!" He says snarky.

"Let's get one thing straight." Ahlesha starts speaking without stepping into the apartment. She sternly starts pointing her finger at Lenox. "I am not your baby. We have a son together and that's it. I will not allow you to jeopardize my relationship with my husband. We are over and there will never be anything more between us. If you ever disrespect me or my husband like that again, you're going to wish that you never meet me."

Lenox started to speak, but Ahlesha cut him off. "Lenox, you have nothing to say. If you're not calling me to speak about the boys, don't call me. This is it."

She walks away and presses the down button hoping that the elevator car would be coming shortly. It seemed like an eternity the forty-five seconds she waited for the car to arrive to the floor.

Lenox stood there watching Ahlesha wait for the elevator. She felt like he was burning a hole in her as she could feel him looking at her. He knew that Ahlesha meant business, and knew that it was time to stop all his antics flirting with Ahlesha. She was happy when the elevator finally came, she got on without looking back at Lenox.

After getting off the elevator she retrieved her car and went home. She prepared dinner for her family. While her and the boys sat at the table waiting for Sean to come home from work she received a text come through her phone. She knew that it was Sean because she had set a special ringtone for his phone calls and text messages.

When she looked at the message, she tried her best to hold back her tears in front of the boys but she couldn't. The message read: *I'm not coming home tonight. I'm still very upset with you and I need some time to cool down. I will*

*be at the Omni Hotel downtown. I will see you when I'm
ready to come home.*

Ahlesha finished feeding the children their dinner, she gave them their baths and put them to bed. She cleaned up the kitchen and retreated to her bedroom. All she could do was pray. She prayed that God would start working on her husband and show him that there was nothing going on between her and Lenox. She also asked God to not allow the devil to tear her marriage apart.

Chapter 16

"So how are you two doing?" Aijah asks Ahlesha as she was home getting ready for a business lunch meeting with Calvin.

"Girl, I guess we're ok. But it is very awkward." Ahlesha sighs.

"Yeah, I bet. Sean really shocked me. I didn't expect him to stay at that hotel for three days. He must have been really mad." Aijah says.

"Yeah, I guess he was."

"But do you really think that Sean believes that you and Lenox were really messing around. I mean, c'mon now, he has to know you better than that." Aijah says as she was trying put on her sexy, black patent-leather stilettos.

"Well I guess he doesn't know me, or either is thinking that history is repeating itself with Lenox and I."

"Oh yeah, I guess he could have been having a flashback."

There was some silence on the phone until Aijah picked back up the conversation.

"Well, we're just going to have to keep praying about this. God will work it out. He knows what's going on."

"Yeah, that's true." Ahlesha decided to switch the subject. "Sooooo, you and this Mr. Perkins are going to have a business lunch meeting, huh?"

"Yes, ma'am. Why did you say it like that?"

"Like what?" Ahlesha replies back.

"Like, implying that the meeting is more than a meeting."

"I didn't say it like that....what? Are you feeling guilty?"

"No. I don't have anything to feel guilty about. It's just lunch." Aijah quickly corrected herself. "A business lunch meeting."

Ahlesha laughed. "Yeah. *A business lunch meeting,* right."

The two ladies ended their phone call while Aijah put the finishing touches on her makeup. After giving herself a once over she did realize that she was a little bit sexy for a business lunch. She had on a pink pencil skirt with a black opaque knit blouse. Though it could have been easily transformed into a business suit if she would have worn the matching blazer that went with the skirt, but she decided to leave it off.

Whether Aijah wanted to admit it or not, she was enjoying being in the presence of another man, who was obviously giving her some attention. She could clearly acknowledge that it was her flesh enjoying all this attention from Calvin. She got into her car and headed toward the fancy restaurant that Calvin suggested that they meet up at.

When she arrived she valets her car and walked into the restaurant. The host greeted Aijah as she walked in the door.

"Hi, welcome to *Maxi's Bistro*, how many will be joining you?" The hostess says.

"Actually, I'm supposed to be meeting someone here." Aijah says as she scans the restaurant for Calvin. "Ahh, I actually see him sitting at the bar." Ahlesha says to the waitress as she points in Calvin's direction.

"Ok, ma'am. Well enjoy your lunch." And she gives Aijah clearance to join Calvin at the bar.

Calvin spots Aijah walking toward him and he rises from his chair to greet her. They both embrace each other with a hug.

"Hey. How are you? You're looking very nice today." Calvin says as he compliments her on her attire.

"Well thank you, Calvin. I'm fine. How are you?" Aijah says as she slightly blushes.

"I'm great. I'm just glad you could meet me on such short notice."

"No problem. The last time we met you had some wonderful news for me, so I couldn't pass up a potential opportunity to hear some more great news."

"So, you're just using me to get ahead in life, huh?"

"No, silly." Aijah lightly swipes Calvin across the arm and they both laugh.

They both walk back up to the hostess area and Calvin asks her to show them to a table so they could be a little bit more comfortable. Calvin makes small talk as they order their food and also shares a few jokes with Aijah. After the laughter dies down Calvin gets into his purpose for inviting Aijah to lunch.

"So first, I want to let you know that Ronda is still making her decision on the consulting position, but I do think it's looking good for you. Ronda is into giving up-and-coming people chances, and the other person that is in consideration has worked with Ronda on a few projects already, so she may not go with her.

Aijah smiles from ear-to-ear when she hears the promising news from Calvin. "That is really great. I was wondering what was going on, but I didn't want to be a pest and call Ronda's assistant. I was just trying to wait patiently to hear something from her."

"Well you know they say, good things come to those who wait?"

"Yeah, I know right."

"Well to get to the other reason why I invited you to lunch is because I will be doing a photo-shoot for *Men's Magazine* and I need someone to pull some styles for me."

"Wow, you're getting a spread in *Men's Magazine*? No offense, but why did they choose you?

Calvin laughs. "Wow. Am I not good enough for the magazine? Am I that ugly?"

"No, I'm not saying that. Actually you're quite handsome. I just didn't realize that you're that high profile to be in such a prestigious magazine." Aijah was a little embarrassed that she came off mean.

"No, no. I understand what you're saying. I know you didn't mean any harm by your comment. Actually the magazine is doing an article on the entertainment business. And they actually want someone to give legal tips on how not to get swindled in the process of becoming a star."

Aijah nods her head. "Oh, ok, I see now."

"I know you may not know, but behind the scenes I'm a pretty big deal amongst the entertainment legal world. Stick around and you'll find out." Aijah gives Calvin a sly look and they continue on with eating their lunch.

After lunch, they still had some time to spare and seeing that they were in the downtown area Aijah asked if he mind doing some window shopping for some possible looks for the magazine spread.

Aijah was a regular at most of the high-end designer stores in the downtown Chicago shopping district of Michigan Avenue. They stopped at stores like Boss, Prada, Gucci, and Neiman's. Many of the retail associates knew

Aijah by first name, as she came in frequently to pull styles for many of her high-profiled clients. Calvin was impressed by the respect she received from the associates. She introduced him to her fashion friends and explained to them the purpose of their visit that day.

The two spent the next three hours looking at styles and talking. Once Aijah looked at the time she realized that she had to meet Anthony to pick up Jason.

"Oh, Calvin, I hate to cut off our time but I must go and pick up my son."

"Ok, no problem."

"I will keep everything in mind of what we liked and disliked and we'll reconvene at a later time."

They both hugged each other and went back to retrieve their cars from the valet at the restaurant.

Chapter 17

After a few weeks went by from the ugly incident with Ahlesha and Sean, they both agreed that it was time for the two of them to seek Godly counsel. Sean being the man of God he is realized that the word of God says, that what God joins together let no man pull it apart. He was going to be the stronger vessel in the marriage and make sure that he and his wife got back on one accord.

They decided to call up Pastor Richards and asked him for some marriage counseling to help get to the root of their marital issues. The ride in the car to the church was silent but not awkward. After having a long talk with one another they knew this was something they both wanted to do. Ahlesha didn't want to lose her husband and Sean loved his wife.

Sean pulls their car into the almost empty parking lot of Temple of Emmanuel. There was an all-black luxury vehicle in the spot designated for Pastor Richards, then there were several other cars parked sporadically throughout the lot – assumed to belong to the church workers that worked in the church throughout the week. As Sean parked and then the two of them get out of the car, Sean quickly walks over to Ahlesha's side of the car to help her the rest of

118

the way out. He then shuts the car door, grabs her hand, then hit the car's key pad to lock the doors of the car. They walk hand-in-hand to the entrance of the church.

When they walk in, no introductions were needed as Temple of Emmanuel was such a family orientated church, that the church secretary knew who Sean and Ahlesha were as soon as they walked in the door.

"Hey, Mr. and Mrs. Alexander! How are you all?" the petite church secretary says.

"We're good! Is Pastor ready for us?" Sean says.

"Yeah, he's ready. He told me to send you all up as soon as you get here."

The secretary signaled to them to proceed to the Pastor's chambers. The two of them were very familiar with the church so they had no problem finding their way. They walk across the sanctuary to a corridor that leads to a stairway. They walk up the stairway and slightly down a hall, and immediately to their left was a door with a sign that read *Office of Pastor J.G. Richards.*

Sean firmly knocks on the door with his left hand as he's still holding Ahlesha's hand with his right. After a few seconds they hear footsteps then the door opens. Pastor Richards opens the door with a huge smile on his face.

"Hey, Sean how do you feel?" Pastor Richard's extends his hand out to Sean. Sean grabs his hand and they both embrace in the manly hand shake/hug.

"Hey, Pastor! I'm doing good, happy to be here with my lovely wife. Wish it could be under other circumstances, but we're here."

"Hey, Ahlesha how are you?" Pastor Richards leans in and gives her a hug. Then he signals them to come into his office.

"I'm well Pastor, thanks for asking."

As they both walk through the threshold of the door Pastor Richards closes the door behind them. Sean and Ahlesha walk over to a couch that was in the Pastor's office and sat down. Pastor Richards then sits down in an oversized-plush chair.

"So you guys are here for counseling? What's going on?"

Sean and Ahlesha both look at each other, waiting on the other to speak, then they both laugh out loud. "Well I'll go first since I'm the one that called, Pastor." Sean says.

"Ok, well c'mon." Pastor Richards responded. Everyone laughed slightly.

"Well….ok…where do I start? My wife and I haven't been on one accord lately. It seems like we've been getting into a lot of arguments lately, and one of the main common denominators seem to be Ahlesha's ex-boyfriend, Lenox." Sean says as he seems to stumble over his words slightly.

"Why is he a problem?" Pastor Richards asked.

"Well apparently he still has feelings for Ahlesha, and I just feel that she wasn't taking the proper steps to stop him from disrespecting our household and me."

Pastor Richards looks over to Ahlesha who was smirking sarcastically. "Ahlesha, do you feel that is true?" He asks.

"No! I don't feel that is true. I've had private conversations with Lenox to let him know that I don't tolerate his blatant disrespectful behavior. However, I believe he was waiting on my non-confrontational husband to put him in his place."

"What do you mean by that?" Pastor Richards asks.

"Yeah, what do you mean by that?" Sean chimes in as well.

"Sean is not a fighter, he doesn't like to argue. He avoids things until he's had enough and then he blows up. Lenox does what he wants to do until he's challenged and then he backs off. Lenox knows this about my husband and I believe he pushed his limits until he couldn't push them anymore."

"So because I don't like to be aggressive that gives him a right to disrespect me?"

"No, I didn't say that. I'm just giving my opinion based on what I know about both of you."

Sean was going to respond, but Pastor Richards interjects. "Ahlesha, have you ever heard the Bible verse in

Proverbs the fourteenth chapter and the first verse saying, a wise woman will build her house, but a foolish woman plucks it down with her hands?

Ahlesha looks at the Pastor in disbelief. "So, now I'm a foolish woman, Pastor?"

Pastor Richards chuckles a little bit. "No, I didn't say that Ahlesha. I'm just merely asking had you ever heard of the Bible verse."

"So then why'd you choose that particular verse?"

"Because I want you to understand a better way to keep the Devil out of your marriage. You must be careful that you give no place to the devil. A wise woman would have seen what Lenox was doing and spoke to him with your husband present to put that fire out. I'm a man and I know how other men operate.

"You're telling Lenox to stop meant nothing to him. But had you told Lenox that with your husband present and Sean being able to back you up would have made more of an impact. Don't take it personal; just use it as a tool if future incidents arise. Always strive to be a wise woman when it comes to your household."

Ahlesha didn't have a response because now she was seeing the situation from a different perspective. She didn't realize that by dealing with Lenox privately, that she was just playing his game with him.

"So he was using me as a pawn to get to my husband?"

"Yes, Eve… I mean Ahlesha." Pastor Richards said as he slyly referenced how Satan got into the serpent in the Garden of Eden to beguile Eve.

Everyone laughed which pulled out some of the tension in the room that started to form when they began to talk about Lenox.

"So, did an incident recently happen to make it so serious that you guys needed counseling?"

They both looked at each other and then Sean spoke. "Yes, Pastor. I actually walked in on them one day at the salon and they were hugging. I sort of lost my temper. Something had been lingering in my mind that I witnessed sometime prior to seeing them hug."

"Well what happened prior?" Pastor Richards asked.

"I was coming home from being out with our boys and when I got home I noticed Lenox's car was in my driveway. So instead of getting out of the car and going in, I parked down the street to see how long it was going to take him to leave me house. It took this man over an hour to leave my house, Pastor." Sean slightly yelled as the memory of the incident made him upset.

"But answer me this, Sean. Why sit in your car and allow the Devil to put false assumptions in your mind as to what was going on? You would have been put at ease if you'd just went inside to see what was going on. Did Ahlesha know that you would be on your way back home soon?"

"Yes, she knew." Sean replies softly.

"So you, too, let the Devil deceive you. Do you really believe that your wife, knowing you would be returning soon, would risk getting caught in a situation in her home?"

"Yeah, Pastor I didn't think about that until you just pointed it out." Sean was humbled by the revelation that was opened up to him. He had allowed the Devil to play mind games with him concerning his wife. He knew that Lenox's motives were unclean, but he allowed the Devil to make him believe that his wife could have unclean motives as well.

"You two must always remember that Satan comes only but to steal, kill, and destroy. He will do whatever he can to put division within your marriage. Never believe that you're one hundred percent in control of your actions because the Devil's forces of deception are very powerful. If he can get you two at odds with one another he will use it as an open door to tear down the marriage." Pastor Richards began to switch subjects. "Ahlesha, name one thing that you would want to change about Sean."

Ahlesha was shocked at the question, she didn't want to answer for fear it would start another argument. "Pastor, do I really have to?"

"Yes, it would help because I'm trying to go somewhere with this."

Reluctantly, Ahlesha gives her answer. "Well if I'd have to change one thing I would have to say that I wish Sean wasn't so boring sometimes." Ahlesha cringed because she felt Sean's eyes staring her down.

"Elaborate on what you call being boring." Pastor said calmly.

"Well, compared to me, Sean is a super-Christian. He thinks everything is a sin and sometimes I feel that he's judgmental. I'm not trying to go to bars or clubs or anything like that, but unfortunately we live in a world that is not majority Christian. Therefore, in order to have fun sometimes we have to be *in the world*, but that doesn't mean we're of the world. I just want to go out on dates and have fun with my husband, but he'd rather stay in the house and watch TV all the time." Ahlesha says.

Pastor Richards was about to give his answer, but Sean eagerly interjected. "Pastor, I'm sorry but I just have to speak my peace." Pastor Richards obliged to him. "First off, I don't think everything is a sin. Many of times Ahlesha is going off her assumption of what I don't want to do and what I'm willing to do. I understand that most places aren't geared to our Christian lifestyle, but it doesn't mean I wouldn't do it if my wife wanted to. Yes, I have my limits but Ahlesha is making more of it than it really is."

125

"So Ahlesha what type of things are you referring to?" Pastor Richards asks.

"Well for example, my cousin was having a party one year for her fortieth birthday and Sean did not want to go. Now I already don't spend time with my family as it is, and you mean to tell me we can't even go to a family member's party – that was at her house, not a club."

"Pastor!" Sean speaks abruptly. "I have nothing against family get-togethers, but this particular cousin is a known weed-head, all her friends are weed-heads and I knew those were the people who were going to be at this party. I didn't want to be around that stuff. Now if it was a party for a more civilized family member, I wouldn't mind, but it's just some situations that I'm not going to subject myself to.

"Well Pastor, he never gave me that reason before." Ahlesha yelled. "He just flat, outright said no when I asked him if he wanted to go. So what was I supposed to think? I thought what I always think, that he was being a stick in the mud."

Pastor Richards spoke before either one of them jumped in. "You see how you two are letting these little misunderstandings and miscommunications set fire to your marriage? You have to learn to stay on one accord in your marriage. You have to learn to outsmart the Devil together, and the only way you do that is by being on one accord

126

spiritually. The devil is never going to play fair, so you have to level the playing field by getting God on your side.

"Stop giving the Devil open doors and he will stop boldly barging his way in. If you two plan on staying married for years to come, then both of you have to start recognizing the Devil. And also gain a better understanding of one another because in some cases you two won't be able to blame everything on the Devil. You two are ultimately in charge of the choices you all make in your marriage." Pastor Richards concluded.

Sean and Ahlesha continued on with their counseling session for another thirty minutes hashing out other issues that they experienced, and the couple left out with a better understanding and weapons to use against their enemy – The Devil.

Chapter 18

One morning as Aijah was sipping her morning coffee while watching little Jason finish his breakfast she faintly heard her cellphone ringing in her bedroom.

"Finish eating your breakfast Jay while I go get my phone." Aijah said as she stood from her chair.

"Ok, Mommy." Jason said with a full mouth of food nodding his head.

As she ran to her room and grabbed her cellphone she looked strangely at the unfamiliar number that appeared on her caller ID display.

"Who could this be?" Aijah says as she pondered the ringing phone. She quickly shrugged off the wonder. She should have been used to receiving calls from strange numbers because of her line of work. "Hello, Aijah Waters speaking." She says as she answers the phone.

"Hi, Mrs. Waters, my name is Sandra, I'm calling on behalf of Shine Bright Productions."

Immediately Aijah felt butterflies in her stomach. Shine Bright Productions was the name of Ronda Shines' production company.

"Yes..." Aijah says intently.

"Yes, I'm calling you on behalf of Ms. Shines to congratulate you on being chosen as our new costume consultant on the new show *Working Girls*."

There was a long pause; Aijah couldn't speak from the shock of the news.

"Mrs. Waters? Are you there?" Sandra said as she was afraid that she may have lost Aijah.

"Yes, I'm sorry, I'm here. I just had a bout of speechlessness. I can't believe I'm having this conversation right now. So much time had gone by I just assumed that Ms. Shines had gone with the other candidate."

"Oh yes, I could understand how you could feel that way. We were consumed with the production of *Slander*. With the show returning for its third season and all the press we're doing, it took Ms. Shines away from focusing on making her decision. She apologizes for not being able to call you personally. She hopes that it doesn't feel impersonal, with me calling you."

"Oh no. I completely understand. I'm just excited to get the call." Aijah says.

"Mommmmyyyyy." Jason sings from the dining room as he feels Aijah has been gone too long. She quickly walks to the room and places her finger over her mouth to signal to Jason to quiet down while she's on the phone.

Sandra continues, "So, production will begin in two months. Ms. Shines will want to meet next week so that she will be able to brief you on the characters' personalities and what she's looking for in terms of style."

As Aijah is intently listening she walks into the kitchen, which is adjacent to the dining room, and grabs a pen and pad out of her junk drawer. She walks back to the dining room and sits back down. She gives Sandra her "uh-huhs" to signal that she's listening. Jason is watching keenly, while finishing off his pancakes as he can feel the energy and excitement coming from his mother.

"Does a meeting next week work for you?" Sandra asks.

"Yes, yes. I will clear my schedule if I have to." Aijah says eagerly.

"Oh no, we don't want you to have to cancel any appointments for us. We understand that you're a busy woman as well. Honestly, Ms. Shines was very impressed with your portfolio and clientele. She loves working with new people, and she knows that with your experience you would have the capability to work with a high-profile team."

Aijah was flattered that Ms. Shines thought that much of her. She started smiling really big; it was getting harder and harder for her to contain the excitement that was radiating out of her. "So, should I just touch bases with you later on this week so we can get a concrete time?"

"Yes, look at your schedule, let me know you're openings and I'll compare with Ms. Shines' schedule. I'm sure we'll be able to put something together." Sandra says.

"Yes, I'm sure, too! Can I just tell you that I'm very excited and I'm grateful for this opportunity – this really means the world to me."

"Thank you. But we should really be the grateful ones. I'm not sure if you know this, but your name carries some weight in Chicago. When we were calling many of the store managers to give them your name to let them know you would be pulling wardrobe for us, we were very surprised that many of them knew you already. We were very impressed I must say."

"Oh wow, well that means a lot to me. Ok, well great! I look forward to setting a time and meeting everyone."

"We look forward to meeting you, too!! Talk to you soon."

Both ladies hang up their phones. Aijah sat in her chair at the dining room table in amazement. She looks at Jason and smiles very big.

"Guess what, Jay?" Aijah says.

"What? Mommy." Jason says in his cute little toddler voice.

"Mommy just got the gig of a lifetime. I'm very, very happy!!"

"Me, too, Mommy." Jason says innocently.

"Awww…" Aijah get out of her seat and goes over to Jason to hug and kiss him. "We have to celebrate! What are we going to do?" Aijah looked at Jason and waited for his response.

"Uhhhh. We can go to the park!" Jason says in his toddler voice.

"The park it is. That will be are celebratory event!"

As Aijah thought about the new beginning she was about to embark upon she knew she had to call Calvin and tell him the great news. She grabbed her cellphone and dialed his number.

As she sat and waited, she peaked over at Jason who was now on the dining room floor playing with his toy truck he'd ran into his room to retrieve.

"Hey, gorgeous!" Calvin says as he picks up the phone, obviously looking at his caller ID seeing Aijah's number.

Aijah blushes slightly. "Hey you. I have some exciting news to tell you."

"I bet I can guess."

"You know?!" Aijah yells out.

"Who do you think drew up the contract?"

"Oh my, God!! Why didn't you tell me?" Aijah screams.

Calvin laughs out loud. "I really wanted to, but I couldn't. That's one of the reasons I'm very successful. I know how to keep business, business and personal, personal."

"I can't thank you enough for recommending me. God is good for allowing you to come across my path. How can I thank you?"

"Hmmm....let me think. We can call it even if you let me take you out to dinner."

Aijah frowns up her face. "Umm, Calvin? Did you forget I'm married?"

"You're actually separated, remember?"

"So what, I'm still married."

"Yeah, you've been separated for over a year now. Don't you think that if you and your husband was getting back together it would have happened by now."

Aijah was tongue-tied. She didn't have a response for Calvin. She never thought about her and Anthony not getting back together, she was still very much in love with Anthony and was hoping for his return. "Look, Calvin I'm not sure if that is a good idea."

"Why not? It's just dinner - dinner with a friend. Two friends celebrating another's victory. How does that sound?"

Aijah pondered Calvin's proposition for a moment. Aijah wasn't going to even front like she didn't want to go out on the date. Although she was waiting on her husband to come back, she didn't mind allowing someone to keep her company in the meantime. "Well you know what? Why not? Sure we can go to dinner." Aijah replied.

"Great, how about tonight?"

"Whoa, slow down. Tonight's not good. I have my son today. How about this weekend? Jason will be with his father this weekend."

"Sounds good to me. I have the perfect restaurant in mind. We'll confirm later on in the week." Calvin says eagerly.

"Ok, great."

They both hang up the phone. After Aijah thought about what she just agreed to, she became a little apprehensive about the dinner. She tried not to make too much of big deal about it because it was only dinner. She felt that it was too much of a reality for her that her marriage could truly be coming to an end and that maybe it was really time for her to move on.

Chapter 19

Aijah had been on a high since getting her great news, however, Calvin bringing up her possible pending divorce sort of put a small dark cloud over her happiness. She decided this particular Wednesday she was going to get to Bible Class early hoping she would be able to get some counseling from Pastor Richards.

She was elated to have been able to get to the church at 5:40 pm, she figured this should be plenty of time for her to get some time in with Pastor Richards. Aijah quickly parked her car, grabbed her purse and Bible bag, and hastily paced to the entrance.

As she walked in she was greeted by the church's secretary who was doing some work on the church announcement board.

"Hey, Sister Waters." She said with a smile on her face while simultaneously looking at her watch. "You're here early…did you come to get some prayer in before Bible Class starts?"

Aijah leans in to give the secretary a hug. "Not quite. I was hoping that I would be able to speak with Pastor Richards." They release their embrace.

"Oh, yeah. Pastor should be sitting on the pulpit in the sanctuary. Go right on in."

"Oh thanks! I was hoping that he didn't have any appointments today. I'm so grateful for his open door policy."

"Yes, we are truly blessed over here at Temple of Emmanuel!"

Aijah ends the conversation and proceeds to walk into the sanctuary to where Pastor Richards was. She loved how the sanctuary looked so angelic when it was empty when no one was inside of it.

Pastor Richards happened to look up from reading his Bible to see who had walked into the sanctuary. He smiled when he saw that it was Aijah. "Is that Aijah?" He says.

Aijah smiled. "Yes, it's me, Pastor. How are you? Do you have some time?"

"I'm great! Yes, I have time for one of my daughters in the Lord. Come on up here and sit with your Pastor."

Aijah walks up the three small steps that lead up to the top of the pulpit. She sat in a chair that was opposite Pastor Richards that was reserved for First Lady Richards.

"Oh, Pastor I'm so happy that you are able to meet with me. I have been having so much going on lately, just needed some time to talk with you to get grounded."

"Ok, well tell me what's going on." Pastor Richards said with concern in his eyes.

"Well first, I actually have some great news. I have been casted as a costume consultant on this new television series, *Working Girls* that will be coming out that is produced by Ronda Shines."

Pastor Richards looks puzzled. "Who is Ronda Shines?"

Aijah chuckled a bit. "You know the shows *Slander* and *Interns and Residents*?"

"Oh yeah, I know those shows."

"Well Ronda Shines created and produced those shows and the one I will be working on."

Pastor Richards seemed impressed. "Oh wow, so this is a pretty big deal?"

"Yes!! To God be the glory!!" Aijah shouted with glee. "Yes, I'm feeling very blessed for this opportunity. It seems like it just fell in my lap. I didn't even know anything about this new show. A friend of mine actually recommended me and I was called in for an interview."

"So God just lined this opportunity up for you, huh? Just make sure you don't get lifted up in it. Stay humble and don't compromise your salvation for the world."

"Yes, Pastor I'm on it. For some reason the Lord have me reading in the Book of Daniel reading about King Nebuchadnezzar and how the Lord tore him down. I don't want to get caught up only to be brought down."

"Oh yes, that is a great story about staying humble." Pastor nods in agreement.

"So, what I really wanted to talk to you about is my current situation with my marriage." Aijah says.

"Yes, I've been praying for you and Anthony."

"Thank you, Pastor... but I've been wondering lately if I should be thinking about filing for divorce."

"How long have you two been separated?"

"For over a year now." Aijah replied somberly.

"A year is a long time. However, what is the Lord telling you to do concerning your marriage?"

"Honestly, Pastor, I don't hear the Lord saying anything. I've been praying about it but I haven't gotten an answer, yet."

"Well that means the Lord wants you to wait."

Aijah gasped in disbelief. "Wait? Wait for what, Pastor? It's clear that the man doesn't want me."

"Well he wants the divorce; let him do the work to divorce you. Don't put your hands in that because you never know what the Lord is going to do. Don't look at this situation with your sight, but you have to walk by faith. Do you still want to be married? Do you want God to fix your marriage?" Pastor Richards asked intensely.

"Yes, of course. I want God to mend our marriage back together."

"Well, take your hands off of it and allow God to work the work. Do you remember how Abraham and Sarah got Ishmael because they decided to put things in their own hands? You don't want to rush out of the marriage before God says that it's over."

"So I'm supposed to sit in this rejected state while he just does what he wants to do. That's not fair." Aijah says perplexed.

"That's because you're looking at it through the flesh. Didn't the Bible say walk by faith and not by sight. Didn't Noah preach 120 years before God brought the flood? Didn't it seem like David wasn't ever going to be king, especially with the enemies that were on his trail, but look at what God did. Don't count God out before he has the chance to perform the miracle." Pastor Richard said smiling.

"So are you saying that you believe God is going to put my marriage back together?" Aijah pressed with hope in her voice.

"I'm saying nothing is too hard for God. He can make a crooked road straight and a rough path smooth." Pastor Richards smiled, again.

Aijah sat there for a moment as she pondered on the words from the man of God. "Pastor, I just don't like this feeling and the way things are going. I feel like I'm stuck and can't move forward in this area of my life. I don't like the limbo I'm in with my marriage."

"The Bible says in Lamentations 3:26 that man should wait, and quietly wait on the salvation of the Lord. You can't worry, mumble, and complain while you wait for the Lord to bless you."

"Pastor that is so true what you said right there. It's easier said than done, though. However, I know if I keep my mind on the Lord, it should be easier to wait, and quietly wait for him to do what he's going to do."

"Yes, if you keep your mind on him, he'll keep you in perfect peace." Pastor Richards says.

"Oh, how I need his peace!!"

The two continued the counseling session until church goers began to pour into the sanctuary for the start of 7:30 pm Bible Class. Aijah felt encouraged that night from the Word that went forth in both the counseling session and Bible Class. Her faith was a little shaky about what the outcome of her marriage would be, but she at least had some courage to keep on in the Lord to see what the end was going to be.

Chapter 20

You have to wait, and wait quietly upon the Lord.
Aijah thought about Pastor Richards' words. It was the
Friday following that Wednesday's counseling session and
she was constantly played the words over in her head as
she sat in the spa. The spa was very busy on this Friday
afternoon, but the busyness didn't stop Aijah from being
engulfed in her thoughts regarding Anthony and the state of
their marriage.

Just as she was reciting some other scriptures and
quotes from Wednesday's meeting Aijah heard the door of
the spa open swiftly. She looks up and sees Anthony burling
toward her. *Wow, what is he doing here?* Aijah thought to
herself. For a second she imagined herself to be in a
romantic love story. Could this have possibly been the
breaking point in Anthony's thoughts concerning their
marriage, and was he coming in to sweep her off her feet
and give her a big manly kiss? Her thoughts continued on.

"Can I speak to you in your office? Now!" Anthony
says angrily.

Aijah's fantasy was quickly doused when she heard
the tone in his voice.

"Sure. What's the problem?" She asked.

"Let's just go in your office." Anthony said even more irritated.

Aijah could tell that Anthony was trying to contain himself of the gasket he was about to blow from whatever was troubling him.

"Connie, can you take over reconciling the appointment book while I go have a meeting in my office?"

"Sure, no problem." Connie says as she gives Aijah a concerned look as they both felt the tension oozing off of Anthony.

They both make their way toward Aijah's office. Anthony was so close to Aijah his energy was basically pushing her down the aisle to the back of the spa to her office. They finally get to her office, and as soon as they step in Anthony lightly slams the door behind them.

"What is the problem?" Aijah yells with concern.

"You emptied our joint account?"

"It's not empty, Anthony." Aijah rolls her eyes.

"Well it might as well be. You only left $75,000 in the bank."

"Anthony most of that money is mine and you know it. I earned that money and I took it out to protect myself. I don't know what you're doing during this separation. Besides, you haven't made a deposit into that account in about eight months. Don't come in here trying to pick an argument with me over nothing."

"I haven't made a deposit because I opened up another account, which I'm sure you have as well."

"Yes, I did. But I'm the only one paying the bills at our house, since you decided to stop paying the mortgage, so I took some money out to help myself...I left you $75,000." Aijah yells.

"Yes, but it was over $300,000 in that account! That was a mutual asset, we are to split half of that account. And I told you if you don't like the situation then you need to divorce me."

"First of all, don't keep throwing the divorce word around like you really want to go there. And don't forget that some of that money is my grandmother's money."

"Aijah, I've been gone for over a year where else do you believe this marriage is headed?" Anthony says with a snarky smile.

"If the marriage is so over than why aren't you divorcing me? Why do you keep putting this on me? And why do you care about how much money I left in that account, we both know that we don't need each other financially." Aijah was trying to change her tone, she was trying to calm herself so she would not say something she didn't mean in the heat of the moment.

"I had plans for that money. I wish you would have consulted with me before you took the money out."

"Well Anthony you lost that privilege when you decided that you didn't want to be married to me anymore." Now Aijah was the one with the snarky smile.

"You're a selfish, bitter woman. Just because I don't want you, you're just being spiteful, now."

Aijah was in disbelief. She put her hands on her hips. "Ha!! You've got to be kidding me. Are you serious? Do you really believe the words that are coming out of your mouth right now?"

"You haven't touched that money for some time now, and all of a sudden you get an unction one day to take $250,000 out of the bank?"

"Anthony, I care not to have this conversation with you anymore. What I do in my life is none of your business right now. Unless you have something you want to talk about concerning Jason, I'm all ears. Other than that, you can see yourself out of my spa."

In Anthony's anger he slams his fist on Aijah's desk. He looked as if he wanted to do more but he reframed himself. He gives Aijah one last stern look, then he turns toward the door, opens it, and walks out.

Aijah stood there in disbelief. She couldn't understand why Anthony was so bent about the money. Anthony had a six figure salary and that joint account wasn't the only money that they had, even when they were together. She knew

Anthony had other money, but was wondering why the money was so important.

Shortly after Ahlesha comes rushing into the office, she closes the door behind her.

"Girl, what was that about?" She asked Aijah in concern.

"Honey, I don't know. He crying about some money I took out our joint account. Some money that I know he doesn't need."

"Well maybe he does if he's making such a big fuss about it."

"Ahlesha, stop it." Aijah say irritated.

"What? I mean come on. I know Anthony has been doing some irrational things lately, but maybe he really needs the money."

"Ahlesha, he doesn't need the money, trust me. He's just trying to get on my nerves. Just something else to torture me with." Aijah sighs.

"Yes, my dear this is one strange case. I've never seen a man act like Anthony. But one thing I do know, whatever it is God will reveal in his time."

"Yes, that's true…"

After that encounter with Anthony, Aijah was becoming more comfortable with her dinner date with Calvin. Although she didn't see it as a romantic date, she still valued her marriage vows. But it was clear to her that Anthony was giving her the go-ahead to act as if she wasn't married to him… and that was exactly what she was intending to do, while keeping it holy of course.

Chapter 21

As the evening drew close Aijah could feel herself becoming nervous of the dinner date. She couldn't believe that she agreed to allow Calvin to come and pick her up. She asked Calvin ahead of time how she was to dress for the date, he simply replied, "like a lady, but comfortable."

She really wasn't sure what that meant, so she chose an outfit that was on the safe side that could be seen as causal, but dressy all in one. She wore some red leggings that had a strip of leather going down the sides of both outer legs, with a black peplum top that was seam-lined in black leather. She finished the look off with her black over-the-knee boots, diamond earrings, necklace, and bracelet set.

When she first looked in the mirror she felt that she was too sexy for a friendly date, the ensemble was something that she would have worn while going on a date with Anthony. But after a few seconds of thinking of Anthony and his recent behavior, she quickly pushed her conscious to the side.

As she sat and waited for Calvin to arrive, which would have been at any moment, she realized that she hadn't put on any perfume. She leaped off the bench that was placed in the foyer of her home and ran into her bedroom. She looked over the abundance of fragrances she had on her dresser. She chose to go with her classic sent of Chanel No. 5. It was her favorite perfume of all times, the scent that made her feel like a lady. She lightly sprayed her neck, wrist, and belly. With Chanel she knew that she didn't need much - a little went a long way.

She went back to her little bench and sat again for a while. She looks at the clock that was placed above the table that was in the foyer across from the bench, it was 7:17. Calvin was almost twenty minutes late from his 7:00 pickup time.

"Maybe he's caught in traffic." Aijah said out loud to herself. She pondered if she should call him, but she didn't want to seem like she was eager for the date, so she just waited. Another ten minutes passed and now she was becoming impatient. She reached into her purse and pulled out her cellphone. Just as she was going through her contact list a call was coming in, it was Calvin.

"Hello?!" She answered irritated.

"Aww man, Aijah. I'm so sorry. I'm pulling up now. I got pulled over for speeding. The officer and I got into a bit of dispute and that's why I didn't call you."

"Oh." Aijah was ready to attack, but couldn't after she heard the excuse from Calvin for why he was late. "Well I'll be right out."

"Ok, great!!"

Aijah grabbed her black jacket, purse and keys and proceeded out of the door. Calvin's car had high-profile lawyer written all over it – he was driving a black, E-Class Mercedes-Benz E250. It was shiny, as if he just got it washed and waxed. Aijah didn't feel impressed as she was used to being around high-profile clients in their luxurious cars.

She locked her front door and walked to the car. Calvin hopped out of the car and ran over to open the door for Aijah. "Your chariot awaits, Mrs. Waters." Calvin says coolly.

Aijah smiled. "Why thank you."

Aijah gets in and sits down, Calvin closes the door and runs back over to the driver side of the car. Aijah notices that Calvin has some old school R&B music playing in the background.

Calvin gets in the car. "Ok. So you ready to have some fun?" He says.

"Yes, let's have some fun." Aijah says with no hesitation.

They soon find themselves in the South Loop area of Downtown Chicago. This was the only thing that surprised Aijah about their date thus far – she just knew that Calvin was going to try to impress her with some swanky restaurant. They pull up to a bustling club-like building. As they pull up to valet the car Aijah could hear the music pumping from the club.

"You brought me to a club? You know I'm a Christian, right?" Aijah says inquisitively.

Calvin laughed out loud. "Yes, Aijah, I know you're a Christian. But this is a restaurant as well. And please I know a lot of Christians that club, too. They're at the club on Saturday, and get right up on Sunday and are sitting in the pew with me." He laughed out loud again.

Aijah rolled her eyes at him. She didn't say another word. She knew this wouldn't be something that she would do all the time, so she just went with the flow...it was just dinner after all.

They walk into the club and then to the hostess area. Because it was so early in the evening there was only a handful of patrons in the club area, most of them only sitting at the bar enjoying the happy hour specials.

"Reservation for Perkins." Calvin says to the hostess.

The hostess scans her list. "Perkins.... Perkins... Perkins. Awww, Perkins. For two?" She says back.

"Yes, for two." He replies.

"Ok. Right this way."

Calvin and Aijah follow the hostess up a flight of stairs that lead out of the club area. When they arrive to the dining area, Aijah was surprised to see this very large banquet area that had at least seventy-five tables in it. She was definitely in a five-star casual restaurant. The hostess showed them to a table and they sat.

"Your waitress, Veronica will be right with you. I hope you enjoy, *Luxe Affair*."

As the hostess walked away Aijah chuckled. Calvin looked at her and chuckled, too. "What's so funny?" He asked.

"I was just thinking, *Luxe Affair*, huh?"

Calvin didn't seem to get the joke. "What? Did I pick a bad spot?"

Aijah shook her head. "Oh, no. I was just thinking about the name of the restaurant. *Luxe… Affair*?"

Calvin was still looking puzzled.

"I'm married and the fact I'm at a place that has the word 'affair' in it is just funny to me, that's all."

"Are you going to keep bringing that up?"

"Excuse me?" Aijah could sense some slight annoyance from Calvin.

"Don't spoil our evening by keep bringing up some guy that doesn't know how to appreciate a good woman. Because if he did, you wouldn't be here with me, you'd be here with him."

"Yeah, I guess you have a point…" Aijah checked herself.

After about an hour and a half of fine dining the two were stuffed.

"Oh my goodness, that was one of the best tasting steaks and sweet potatoes that I've ever tasted in my life. I've never had gourmet soul food before." Aijah said as she looked at her plate wanting to lick it.

"Yes, wasn't it good? I like to call myself a restaurant connoisseur, so when I heard about this place I just had to try it."

"This is your first time here?" Aijah says shockingly.

"Yes. I was looking for the perfect date to bring here."

"Ha!" Aijah takes her napkin, wipes her mouth, and throws it down on top of her plate. "Very charming. Cut it out, Calvin."

"What?!" He says as he throws his hands in the air.

"This was just supposed to be a celebratory dinner, remember. This isn't a date. Friends, right?"

Calvin stares at Aijah for a moment. "Yeah, friends."

They share a stare between eyes. For the first time Aijah was realizing that she was becoming attracted to Calvin.

"So, you want to go downstairs and just hang out for a while?" Calvin asks Aijah.

"Sure, why not?"

Calvin summons over the waitress and asks for the check and a VIP table downstairs in the club area.

After Calvin pays the bill and the hostess walks them down to their table in the club area. By now the club was in full dance party mode. The urban music was loud and infectious. As they got comfortable, a VIP waitress came over to take their drink order.

"Hi! What can I get you two tonight?" The young pretty waitress says.

"I'll take a glass of wine – do you have any chardonnay?" Calvin asks.

"Yes, we do. Our house wine is very delicious." She replies.

"Ok, great, that's what I'll have."

"And you my lady." The waitress says to Aijah.

"I'll have a San Pellegrino with limes, please." Aijah replies.

"Ok. I'll be right back."

After the waitress walks away Calvin looks puzzled. "What? Don't tell me you don't drink either?" He says.

"That's right, Calvin, I don't drink. Is that a problem?"

"No, just find it shocking."

"Why is it so shocking?" Aijah asks.

"It's just in this line of business we both work in, you just make assumptions about people, and it's not often that someone shocks me and proves me wrong."

Aijah scrunches up her forehead and raises her eyebrows. "So what was your assumption of me? That I was a drunk?"

Calvin laughs. "No. I didn't think you were a drunk. But you're always so professional during our meetings, and when I see you at professional events you're always reserved. I just knew that when I caught you in a more private setting that you would let your hair down."

"So are you saying I'm boring?" Aijah says with a smile.

"No, far beyond boring. Just a different type of woman… one that I'm not accustomed to, that's all."

"Uhhmmmm…." Aijah replies.

The waitress finally brings their drinks over and they people watch for about another hour or so. Calvin ended up having only two glasses of wine, as he said that he didn't feel comfortable drinking alone.

They got up from their table and went outside to retrieve Calvin's car from valet. The car ride back to Aijah's house was quiet. They had had a great evening, Aijah admittedly was enjoying the company. They pull up to Aijah's house, Calvin cuts his car off and walks Aijah to her door.

As they approach the door, she unlocks it and they both step into the foyer. It was some awkward silence for a moment.

"So how about a coffee night cap?" Calvin says.

Aijah looks up at the clock that was above the table in her foyer. *11:37 pm.* She thought to herself as she looked at the clock. Apprehensive, yet still enjoying the company, she invited Calvin in.

She led Calvin into her den and gave him the remote. "See if you can find something on TV."

"Ok." He says as he turns on the TV.

Aijah goes into the kitchen and preps the coffee machine for a pot of coffee. She returns back to the den and sits on the sofa near Calvin. Just like a man he turned to ESPN to see what was going on in the sports world.

"You have a nice home." He says as he takes his eyes off the screen and glazes over the portion of the house he could see from where he was sitting.

"Thank you. I did a lot of the decorating myself."

"Well you're very creative. Styling is definitely your forte."

As they sat longer they both could smell the aroma of the coffee brewing with the timer signaling that the coffee was ready shortly behind it.

"Coffee's ready!" Aijah says chipper as she gets up from the sofa. Calvin follows suit and walks to the kitchen with her. "How do you like your coffee?" She asks Calvin.

"Just cream." He responds.

"Really? Same here. I have French vanilla, caramel mocha, and mint chocolate. Which one do you like?"

"Uhhhh... I'll take the French vanilla."

Aijah goes into the refrigerator pulls out the French vanilla and caramel mocha liquid creamer. She slides the French vanilla creamer over to Calvin, as she opens up the caramel mocha and pours a splash into her mug.

After Calvin prepares his coffee he takes a sip. "Wow. You can make a great cup of coffee."

"Thanks." She laughs. "My husband used to say the same thing." She catches herself. "Oops. Sorry. Can't help it, that slipped out."

Calvin shrugs his shoulders. "Don't worry about it."

They take their coffee and head back to the den. They engage in more conversation, Aijah talks about Jason and Calvin talks about growing up in a house full of sisters. As the evening went on they find a movie to watch. Aijah got more comfortable and got slightly closer to Calvin. They were really enjoying watching the movie *Love Jones*.

Sometime later Aijah began to feel a strange sensation near the small of her back right above her butt area. She hadn't realized that they both dozed off while watching the movie. She didn't remember how she ended up laying on Calvin's chest while he was laying back on the couch. In the mist of his sleep his hand found its way perusing Aijah's soft body. Aijah slightly opened her eyes and saw that the time was 2:14 am. Her relaxed state kept her on Calvin's chest as her flesh was enjoying the feeling of Calvin's caressing.

It had been awhile since she felt the sensual touch of a man next to her. Calvin realizing that Aijah was awake added a little more pressure to his touch as he felt she was obliging to his advances. Soon he was giving her soft pecks on her forehead, which lead down to her lips.

Before she knew it they were in a full grope session right there in her den on the couch that her and her husband had plenty of love sessions on.

Once she popped into the reality of what was going on, she hopped up and released her lips from Calvin's.

"Oh my, God. I'm sorry!" She then covered her mouth with her soft pink colored manicured hands.

"What's the matter?" Calvin says.

"Calvin, this is a little too close for comfort for me. You gotta go."

"Wait, wait." Calvin says as the moment was now becoming awkward and uncomfortable. "I'm sorry. Did I advance too much?"

"Yes, but it's not all your fault. I can't act like I didn't like it or want you to."

"Then why are you putting me out?" Calvin asked.

"Calvin, you know why. This isn't right. Just leave and we'll talk about this another time."

Calvin got up from the sofa grabbed his jacket and Aijah ushered him out of the house. She watched from the window as he got in his car and drove off. Aijah wanted him to hurry up and leave her house because she felt hormones waking up that she should have been trying to keep dead. She was still a married woman and she didn't want adultery on her resume.

Chapter 22

A couple of weeks went by after Calvin and Aijah's rendezvous. He had been texting and calling her, but she would conveniently miss his call. She was happy that in her meeting with the production team for *Working Girls* that he wasn't present. Aijah was embarrassed at how she kicked Calvin out of her house, but she knew she wanted to keep her salvation. She was upset with herself that she let her guard down that low to get put in that temptation.

However, the remnants of the evening were still with her. She was sitting at the front desk of the spa going over the appointment book fighting the flashbacks that were trying to creep back in her mind. Every single time she saw herself kissing Calvin she felt tingles shooting throughout her body. Although she hadn't had sex with him, she felt like she committed adultery against her husband.

As she sat at the front desk Ahlesha comes over to her to hand her the phone. She hadn't even realized that the phone rang.

"Who is it?" She asks Ahlesha.

"Mr. Calvin Perkins." She says with a smile.

She started waving her hands no and shaking her head. "Noooooo. Tell him I'm not here." She whispered.

Ahlesha put her hand over the phone's voice receiver. "I can't do that I already told him you were here." She whispered back.

"Well tell him I'm busy." Aijah whispers again.

"Girl, just take this phone. I'm not about to play these games with you." Ahlesha sat the cordless phone down on the desk and walked away.

Aijah picked up the phone and covered the voice receiver. "Shows how much of a friend you are." Aijah yells to Ahlesha.

"Whatever!" Ahlesha yells back.

Aijah took a deep breath. "Aijah Waters speaking." She speaks into the phone.

"Hi, how are you Mrs. Waters?" Calvin says in his sexy deep voice.

Instantly Aijah gets a flashback, she cringes in her seat. "I'm good, how are you Mr. Perkins?"

"I'm fine, but for some reason I get a feeling that you're avoiding me."

"Avoiding you? Why would I be doing that?"

"Seriously, was it that bad that you can't talk to me anymore?"

"So you just go right into, huh? No warm up or nothing?"

"I'm a lawyer, what do you expect. Now come on, talk to me."

Aijah sighs. "Look Calvin. I take my salvation very seriously. I allowed myself to be caught in a weak moment and I just don't want it to happen again."

"Well if you'd just talk to me then we can get an understanding. I'm not going to even begin to act like I understand all this 'salvation' talk and your strict relationship with God, but I do have enough sense to respect a woman's wishes when it comes to intimacy."

Calvin expressing that put her slightly at ease concerning their encounter. She wasn't sure if the incident was going to cause some friction or uncomfortableness between the two, especially seeing that they would be working together on the show.

"Calvin, I do want us to remain friends. I just needed a moment to collect myself."

"That's alright with me. I can't lie and say that I don't like you or are not attracted to you. But if your wish is to take it slow, I will surrender to it. Okay?"

"Okay." Aijah says back.

They converse back and forth for a little while longer then they ended the call. When Aijah hung up the phone and put it back down on the desk, little did she know that Ahlesha was waiting in the background for her to get off the phone so she could get all into her business.

"So what was that all about?" Ahlesha says as she rushes over to Aijah.

"I knew your nosy self wouldn't be too far behind."

"Whatever. What's up with you and Mr. Lawyer?" Ahlesha says as she leans on the desk, grabbing a grape from the bowl of grapes Aijah was eating from. She pops one in her mouth and starts chewing.

Aijah sighs. "Girl, I let him get a little bit too close a couple of weeks ago, and we had a close call."

"What?" She yelled out in surprise.

Everyone in the spa stopped what they were doing and looked up at the two of them.

Aijah stood up and grabbed Ahlesha by the hand and they walked back to her office.

"Get in here with your big mouth self." Aijah pulled Ahlesha into the office and closed the door. "Sit down."

"So what happen? How close did you get?" Ahlesha was at attention.

"Well we kissed and had a little groping."

"Whaaatttt. Did your clothes come off?" Ahlesha asked.

"No! I didn't let it get that far."

"Oh. Well girl just be careful. But personally I don't see anything wrong with you getting to know someone else. It ain't like Anthony is showing any signs of wanting to get back with you."

"So that means I should jump right into the arms of the first man that shows me a little attention. I don't think so.

We're not even close to divorcing. So I can't even allow myself to think about being in another relationship."

"So what you're going to be an old maid?"

"Why does that mean I'm going to be an old maid? I still love my husband. But really, c'mon now, I think that says a lot about me if I get into another relationship before I know where my current one is going."

"You do know where the current one is going…nowhere." Ahlesha replies.

"Shut up, Ahlesha!" Aijah rolls her eyes. "Get out of my office I don't want to talk about this anymore."

Ahlesha gets up and starts laughing. "Ha, ha. Don't worry about me. I'll leave. But do know I've been kicked out of better places than this."

Aijah picks up a piece of paper, balls it up and throws it at Ahlesha as she's leaving out of the office.

Chapter 23

After Calvin and Aijah's talk their friendship had begun to get back to a normal state. Production was in full motion and they were having more and more frequent meetings with one another. They were becoming very close friends. They hadn't had any new intimate encounters, but Calvin was soon becoming Aijah's male confidant. Anthony was beginning to fade far from her mind.

"Ok, everyone that's a wrap!" The assistant director said while they were on set for *Working Girls*.

As the actors and production team disbursed into their small groups Calvin walked over to Aijah while she was at the food service table.

"You want to go and get some real dinner?" Calvin said as he saw Aijah search for something good to eat.

She looked up. "Hey!" She gave him a hug. "Yes, I would love to. I'm so sick of eating this same food, I would love a decent dinner."

"Ok, well I'll go get my car and meet you out front." Calvin said.

"Great, let me go over something with Ronda, I'll get my bag and be right out."

They finally got in the car and went to a nice sit down Italian restaurant. The restaurant was very casual and unassuming. Calvin and Aijah were talking about the show and going over how happy they were that the show was taking off.

As they were speaking Aijah stops talking and appeared to have her eyes fixated on something or someone.

"What's the matter?" Calvin says, as he tried to look in the direction that Aijah was looking in to see what had Aijah's attention. Calvin then looks up and then realized that he saw Anthony walking in their direction. He recognized his face from the big wedding picture that Aijah had in her den from his frequent visits to Aijah's home.

As Anthony drew closer, Calvin stood up – Aijah just leaned back in her chair and folded her arms. When Anthony reached the table, Calvin extended his hand to give Anthony a handshake. "Hey, man how's it going?"

Anthony was outdone at Calvin's audacity to want to shake his hand like they were buddies. He then looks at Aijah. "So is this your little boyfriend?" He says with a smirk on his face. Calvin was still standing there with his hand extended, but Anthony never reached back to shake it.

"No. This is my friend, Calvin. We work together."

Anthony then looked at Calvin and then back to Aijah. Calvin put his hand down, now realizing that Anthony wasn't going to shake it. Calvin sat back down.

"So, what's going on with you? And where's my son?" He says aggressively.

"Our son is with Ahlesha's mom. And nothing much is going with me."

"So you stop praying for me?" Anthony says.

Aijah looks at him strangely, and Calvin whose head was down, looked up with the same strangeness.

"I don't know what you mean." Aijah says.

"You stopped praying for me. I don't feel your prayers anymore."

Aijah leans back in her chair again and folds her arms. "Well, that quite funny, I didn't think you cared if I was praying for you."

"Who wouldn't want their wife to pray for them? So you don't care anymore?"

"What, Anthony? Where is all this coming from?"

Calvin is disgusted, but not surprised because he's a man he understands where Anthony is coming from. He knew that the fact that Anthony was seeing Aijah in the presence of another man would evoke that natural jealously that's in every man, whether he wanted to admit it or not. But Calvin wasn't going to let him swoop back in and ruin what he'd been working on for months.

"Anthony, I understand this is your *wife* and all, but we're having dinner. And you've showed for almost two years…" He turns to Aijah, "Two years right, baby?" He turns back to Anthony, "Two years that you don't care if your *wife* is still praying for you."

Aijah could feel the testosterone rise in the room. "What a minute, y'all." She says.

"Look, man. Contrary to what you think, don't question me about my conversation with my wife."

Calvin then stands up. "I'm trying to be nice, but for real, I think you need to see your way out of this restaurant. You can talk to your wife on your own time."

Aijah could see that Calvin was only trying to aggravate Anthony by his choice of words. She then stand ups. "Calvin, stop it." She says as she looks at him. "Let me have a few words with my husband, please."

She then walks around from behind the table and then grabs Anthony by the arm and walks him out of the restaurant.

The crisp, cool, fall air catches her off guard as she didn't grab her jacket in the heat of the moment of the situation. Anthony realizing she was cold took off his jacket and put it around her shoulders. "Thank you." She says.

"Hey, I'm sorry."

"No you're not!" Aijah says aggravated. "What do you think you're doing?! You don't want me, haven't shown that you want me, but yet you're jealous cause I'm having dinner with someone?"

"Are you on a date?"

"Anthony! What does that matter to you? Do you want to be married to me?!!" Aijah yells, Anthony didn't respond. "Exactly! No answer, so that would be a no!"

Anthony still didn't respond.

"You know what? You can get out of my face and stop playing games with my heart. Coming in here only to send me on this stupid emotional rollercoaster. You need to figure out what the heck you want. Stupid male ego. You make me want to slap you!"

Aijah flung the jacket off her shoulders and forcibly pulled open the restaurant door and went back in to sit with Calvin.

"You ok?" Calvin says with concern.

"No!" Aijah yells.

"I apologize for my male ignorance."

Aijah didn't say anything. She was fuming. Calvin then gets up and then sits on her side of the table in the other chair next to her. He puts his arm around her. "Don't let it upset you. Us men we're stupid sometimes."

Aijah removes Calvin's arm from around her. "I just don't appreciate him playing with my feelings like that. And you..."

Calvin puts his hands up in surrender. "Hey, I said I was sorry."

"But you should know better. What if y'all would've gotten into a full-on brawl with your instigation?"

"Hey, I'm a lawyer, I can't help it." He then smiles at Aijah.

"Not an excuse, and not cute." She then stares at him for a while, and then starts laughing herself.

They went back to eating their semi-cold dinner. While Aijah was playing around with her food she began to think. "Calvin, from a man's perspective do you think the reason Anthony got upset was because he may have been thinking of working things out?"

"Naw, it's just the male ego. Like you said, he's just trying to play with your emotions and your heart."

Calvin wasn't about to give her his real answer. He wasn't about to put Aijah right back into Anthony's hands. They had been getting very close. In Calvin's mind he was only trying to set himself up to be next in line for Aijah when she finally divorced from Anthony. He had started to go to church and been behaving himself just enough for Aijah to keep him around. Anthony had messed up and Calvin was doing everything he could do to capitalize on Anthony's screw up.

"I know. But I can't help but think it's more to this incident that just the male ego." Aijah then puts both elbows on the table and sinks her face into the palms of her hands.

"Aijah, don't let it fool you. Take it from a man. Don't be naïve." Calvin was hoping that he was steering her back toward him and not toward Anthony.

Aijah was contemplating the entire event. She wasn't sure what to think. She knew very well that it could be the male ego, but what if Anthony was sending up smoke signal and was trying to get Aijah to come in to rescue their failing marriage.

Chapter 24

It appears that Anthony wasn't sending up smoke signals…at least that's the way it appeared to Aijah. Another year had gone by, Aijah's career continued to flourish but her love life continued to be a soap opera. Aijah wrapped up the first season of *Working Girls* and was entering into another season.

Due to the success of the show and Aijah's name being linked to the amazing styling of the A-list celebrities, Aijah was getting a plethora of new clients and the spa's business was booming. The business became so good that Aijah gained enough capital to open a spa in New York City.

Surprisingly Calvin was still hanging in there with Aijah as well. Although, there friendship still hadn't grown beyond being just friends Calvin still had some hope in his mind. For Aijah, she found herself passing the time with Calvin. Her marriage was still in limbo and neither of them still hadn't filed for divorce yet.

Aijah was off to New York City for the grand opening of Posh Studios number two. Of course Ahlesha, being her business manager, joined her and Calvin came along for the ride. It had been a hectic day from getting up at 5:00 am to catch their plane from Chicago to New York City.

The crew barely got a chance to relax once arriving at LaGuardia Airport. They had to rush to the spa to make sure everything was in line for the grand opening and all of the business issues were squared away. Aijah barely got thirty minutes to rest at the hotel before it was time for her to get glammed up for the grand opening party.

Aijah met Ahlesha and Calvin in the hotel lobby. "Hi, guys you ready?" She asked.

"Yes, I'm ready and excited!!" Ahlesha proclaimed. Ahlesha was loving being able to hob-nob with some of the celebrities she was getting a chance to meet through Aijah's connections.

Calvin nodded and all three walked out of the hotel to the awaiting town car. The car ride was short, as the spa was only about ten blocks away from the hotel. As soon as they arrive the paparazzi was overwhelming. The press was even more frenzied than at the Chicago grand opening. The crew posed with dozens of celebrities and were getting questions asked from left and right. Aijah and Ahlesha didn't know what to do they were being pulled in so many different directions.

Finally the crew was able to go inside to greet the guests, to which Aijah was met with a round of applause from everyone. She was truly humbled by the experience.

After Aijah mingled with a few people, she dipped off to a quiet corner with Calvin to watch the party from a distance. She laughed at Ahlesha as she watched her get as many hugs and pictures of celebrities as she could.

Calvin was just standing there smiling at Aijah. "I'm very proud of you." He says.

"Thanks, Calvin. I'm proud of myself. I never envisioned myself blowing up like this. I thank God that I met you and that he put it on your heart to refer me for the job on *Working Girls*."

"Honestly, I know you may think that the only reason I referred you for the job is because I liked you, but seriously I really thought you would be great for the job."

As Aijah was standing there smiling at Calvin's compliment a very popular celebrity walked up to the couple. Aijah couldn't believe who it was.

"Aijah Waters?" The celebrity said.

"Yes, yes." She extended her hand to shake hers. "Oh my God, I can't believe it's Kelsey Spencer." She looked at Calvin and was smiling from ear to ear.

Kelsey Spencer was a popular R&B singer who was blowing up around the world and her coming to Aijah's grand opening was a really big deal.

"Hi, I just wanted to come over here and say congratulations. I absolutely love your spa. I visited incognito to your Chicago spa several times."

Aijah was stunned. "Really you've been to Posh Studios Chicago? Why didn't you tell me? You know we have a VIP lounge for our celebrity guest?"

"I know, but sometimes I like to go as a regular person to see how I would be treated if people didn't know I was 'KJ', you know what I'm saying?"

"Yeah, I get it, but you know our motto is that we treat every client like a celebrity?"

"Yes, I know. Why do you think I've come back on several occasions?"

Everyone laughed and they continued in the conversation.

"Please, please, next time you come please let me know so that we can give you your VIP treatment, and it will be on the house – whatever you want."

"Ok you got it!"

"Great!" Aijah exclaimed.

"Your ideas are great. Have you ever thought about getting your own spa line?" Kelsey Spencer asked.

"Yes, I have but the process is so tedious and time consuming."

"Well actually I have someone that I can connect you with. I think you should really think about doing that to enhance your brand." Kelsey said.

Aijah was jumping up and down with glee. "Aww, thanks I appreciate it."

174

"One other thing… I noticed at the spa you didn't serve alcohol. I think that would be one thing that would send your business over-the-top."

Aijah didn't like the way the conversation was shifting. Aijah's religious beliefs prevented her from serving alcohol in her establishment. She didn't drink and didn't want to serve it to her customers. As Aijah thought, she was trying to find a way to say nicely to Kelsey Spencer that she'll pass on her suggestion. Aijah didn't want to compromise what she believed in just to impress some celebrity.

"Well honestly Kelsey…" Aijah proceeded cautiously. "I just choose not to serve alcohol. I don't drink and feel like my services are just as fine without the added alcoholic beverages." Once Aijah got it off her chest she felt at ease. She actually cared more that she stood to her beliefs and cared less about what Kelsey Spencer thought.

"Well you're right. It is your spa, and that's just probably the drinker in me that is speaking. It was only a suggestion, anyway."

After much mingling the grand opening party was finally over, the crew was exhausted and hurried back to their hotel rooms to get some sleep before the next day's flight.

The next morning they all got up to go to breakfast before their 1:30 pm flight. They all meet in the hotel restaurant. They were seated and immediately a waitress came over to take their orders. As they were sitting waiting on their food Ahlesha made a crazy face as she was looking at her phone.

"Oh my!!" She said, then she started smiling.

"What?" Aijah said. Calvin looked on, as he too wanted to know what the excitement was about.

Ahlesha tapped her phone and then handed it to Aijah. Aijah's mouth dropped to the floor as she read the headline of the picture that she saw. "Chicago spa owner posing with boyfriend at NYC grand opening." As soon as she was done looking at the picture she showed it to Calvin. Once he read it all he could do was smile.

Ahlesha just happened to be checking the Chicago local news stories when she stumbled upon headline. She grabbed her phone back to look at the headline again.

"What do you think Anthony is going to say when he sees this?" Ahlesha asked.

"You know what? I don't even care. I feel like a fool. It's been three years since we've been separated with no sign of reconciliation. Why am I still holding on?" Aijah yells.

"Yeah, maybe it is time to move on." Calvin chimes in.

"Well you didn't say that he had been calling lately, talking about nothing." Ahlesha says.

Calvin sharply looks at Aijah. "Anthony has been calling you? You didn't tell me that."

"Well he's been calling about nothing. Lately I've been getting these random calls from him. All he's been saying is that I'm a great mother and was a great wife. He was happy to have had the opportunity to have a son with me. But he never mentioned getting back with me."

"Aijah, I thought we were better than that. Why didn't you tell me?" Calvin says visibly hurt.

"Calvin, what I discuss with my husband is between him and me. I don't have to tell you everything."

"Oh wow. I see." He says disappointed.

Calvin gets up from the table and walks off. Calvin didn't know how to express that he was hurt because he has been waiting in the wings all this time, and the thought that his waiting appeared to be in vain bothered him.

"He'll be ok." Aijah says as she watches Calvin walk away.

"Are you sure? He seems pretty hurt."

"He'll be ok, Ahlesha. Besides, this is not about him. I'm the one stuck in the middle and don't know what to do. I'm the one dealing with a confused fool, who claims he doesn't want to be married to me but won't file the divorce. So as for Calvin he can get over himself." Aijah says nonchalantly.

"Yeah, I hear you, girl." Ahlesha says.

The plane ride back to Chicago was uncomfortable and full of tension needless to say. Aijah felt slightly bad after a while that she'd hurt Calvin's feelings, but the incident was unavoidable.

Chapter 25

After the three of them came back from New York City, Aijah could tell that Calvin had hit his final straw with their unofficial, official love triangle. Calvin barely was speaking to Aijah and he didn't want to have their usual dinner and lunch dates that they would normally have.

Aijah knew it was time to make some decisions in her life concerning her marriage. Three years was long enough and she knew she either needed to make one last attempt to reconcile with Anthony or go to the court house and file for divorce.

She remembered her conversation with Pastor Richards about waiting on the Lord, but she just couldn't see the Lord telling her to wait three years or even longer to see if her husband was going to get himself together. She felt like this portion of her life was at a standstill and she didn't want it to be that way any longer.

She contemplated long and hard and began to do her research about divorcing in the state of Illinois. She knew that they had past the two year separation time frame, but unfortunately she knew that they didn't have real cause for divorcing – other than irreconcilable differences.

Subconsciously, she'd made up in her mind that she was ready to file for divorce. She knew that she should consult with Pastor Richards, but she didn't want him to steer her away from the decision that she'd already decided to do.

While Aijah was sitting at her desk at the spa she yelled out to Ahlesha. "Hey, Ahlesha come here for minute."

Shortly after Ahlesha appeared in the doorway. "Yeah, what's up?"

"Are you busy?" Aijah asks.

"No. What's up?"

"Come on in and close the door."

Ahlesha stepped in the office and closed the door behind her. She sat down in the leather chair in front of Aijah's desk. "Uh, oh. What's the problem?"

Aijah exhaled. "Nothing, but I think it's time for me to file for divorce."

Ahlesha's mouth flung open. "Really, Aijah!! You're ready to do it?"

"Yes, I think so." She says as she shakes her head up and down.

"Wow. I must say that I never thought this day would come. I mean I know I joked around about you moving on, but I've been praying for you two. I don't want my friends to divorce."

"Yeah, I know. But I really feel that it's time to let it go. It's been three years. Why am I still holding on to this dead weight?"

"Wow." Was all Ahlesha could muster up to say.

"Yeah… I know, right?"

The two ladies sat there silently until Ahlesha spoke. "Well God will have someone better for you. Maybe it's Calvin?"

Aijah chuckled. "Truth be told. I like Calvin, but I don't see him being the one. I know he wouldn't be truly committed. He don't want God for real, it's me that he wants. And if it's anything I learned from you and Lenox is don't try to date a man that's not on the same page as you are."

"Yeah, I learned that lesson the hard way didn't I…almost missed out on my man." Ahlesha said.

"I hate that I feel like I've strung him along all this time. He didn't deserve that. Although we've come to become good friends, I believe the friendship is based on what he believes will happen in the future for us. You know what I mean?"

"Yes, I completely understand." Ahlesha looked so sad as she spoke to her friend about her impending divorce. "Well are you going to talk to Anthony about it before you go and file?"

"I don't know. I guess he should be expecting it seeing that he keeps putting the filing in my hands. What would there be to discuss with him?"

Ahlesha shrugged. "I guess you would be telling him that you realize it's time and figure out how you all are going to divide everything. I guess. I mean you don't want to have an ugly split and make enemies out of each other." Ahlesha's face became pouty as she looked on her friend's somber face.

"Yeah, maybe I'll stop by his office tomorrow while Jason is at school. Maybe I'll take him to lunch and we can talk about it?"

"Yeah, sounds like a good idea, that way you'll be able to ease into the conversation."

Silence rang throughout the room again. Aijah just seemed to be staring into space until she spoke again. "Who knew that there would be so many bouts of uncertainty that came with marriage? I don't think I was prepared for my marriage to go in this direction. I really thought my marriage would last forever." As she allowed those last words to slip from her lips she felt her emotions over take her.

Throughout the entire three years Ahlesha saw a strong, fearless woman in Aijah. She never saw Aijah breakdown or cry concerning her marriage. Aijah had been a strong rock, planted firmly on God - putting it all in his hands not worried much about her marriage. But finally Aijah broke down. She released all the strength that she had concerning what God was able to do for her.

Her letting go was not about losing faith in God, but she was letting go and respecting that God wouldn't go over man's boundary. She knew that God could turn the situation around, and believed that God dealt with Anthony about coming back to his family. She knew at the end of the day Anthony had to be the one to yield to doing what was right...that was the part Aijah was letting go of. Letting go of the hope that Anthony would change his mind.

Chapter 26

"Ok, baby, have a good day." Aijah said to Jason as she dropped him off at school. She walked back to her car, got in and sat down. Once again, those butterflies had made their arrival back in her belly. She knew she was beginning a process that she couldn't turn back from, but she knew it was time to do it.

She turned the ignition to her car and drove off to Anthony's office in the South Loop. Once arriving she parked her car in the building's parking garage and quickly walked toward the elevator. The elevator arrived shortly after she pressed the down button, she stepped on and pressed the lobby button. She found herself tapping her feet to the beat of the elevator music, thereafter, she arrived to the lobby floor.

She got off the elevator and the security guard greeted her as they were aware of whom she was. She walked down the hall and finally arrived at Anthony's office suite of his investment company.

When she walked in she was greeted with a strange look from the receptionist. "Hi, Mrs. Waters, can I help you?" She said.

"Hi, Carmen! Is Anthony here, I'd like to take him to lunch."

"Uhm, Mrs. Waters, Anthony hasn't been to the office for a week. He's been calling in sick." Carmen couldn't understand why Aijah didn't know the whereabouts of her husband. Contrary to what Aijah believed, Anthony didn't share the current status of his marriage with anyone on his staff.

"Really?" She stood there for a moment. "Ok. Well thank you, Carmen."

Aijah was dumbfounded. She hadn't realized Anthony was sick, but then again she did realize that she hadn't see him because he had been having the part-time nanny come and pick up Jason. Aijah walked out of the office and went back to her car.

"I'll just drive over to his house." She said out loud to herself as she got in the car and started it up.

She rushed over to his house and parked on the street. "Yep, he's here. His car is here."

She quickly got out and briskly walked to his front door. She ranged to door begin vigorously. Shortly a woman came to door, she appeared to be a nurse - Aijah assumed by her nurses outfit. The lady appeared to recognize Aijah when she laid eyes on her.

"Uhm, is Anthony here?" Aijah said intently as the woman had thrown her off guard.

185

"Yes, Mrs. Waters he's here."

Again, Aijah is dumbfounded that the lady not only knew her, but knew her name as well.

"Come on in Mrs. Waters." She stepped back from the doorway to allow Aijah space to come in.

Aijah stepped in the door and was very nervous. She didn't know what she was walking into. She then followed the nurse up the stairs to Anthony's bedroom. When she walked in she almost passed out in shock.

Anthony looked very sickly; he had IV tubes coming out of his arms and seemed to had lost a considerable amount of weight.

"Anthony!" Aijah yelled. "What is going on?" Aijah stared at Anthony, then at the nurse.

"Mrs. Waters, calm down. He's ok. Just a little winded from his chemo treatment today. But he'll be ok."

"Chemo?! What do you mean chemo treatment? He has cancer?!" Aijah yelled at the nurse.

Anthony began to slightly squirm in his bed. He was too weak to react to Aijah's finding out of condition.

"Come with me Mrs. Waters." The nurse grabbed Aijah by the hand and took her into the guest room that was next door.

Once seated Aijah yelled out. "How long as he had cancer?"

"About three years now, Mrs. Waters?" The nurse said calmly.

"Three years? Three years?" She chuckled in disbelief. "He hasn't had cancer for three years. You must be mistaken."

"Unfortunately Mrs. Waters it's true. I've actually been taking care of him for about a year now. When he first found out about the colon cancer the doctors were able to treat it aggressively, but the cancer was really tough. They were able to get it all and it went into remission for about six months but then it came right back and appears to have spread to one of kidneys."

Aijah was taken aback. She was now thinking about how she noticed when Anthony had went bald and cut off all his facial hair. She now understood it was because of the chemo and radiation treatments.

After the nurse was able to calm Aijah down, she took Aijah back into Anthony's room and sat her by his bed side. Aijah sat there and a rush of compassion came over her for her ailing husband. She was angry with Anthony for keeping from her that he had cancer. But she couldn't say much because by now he'd fallen asleep, and soon after she did too.

After a while, Aijah was awakened by Anthony calling her name.

"Aijah... Aijah... wake up."

Aijah was leaned back in the Lazy Boy sofa sleeper that was adjacent to Anthony's bed. As she came to she quickly sat up, wiped her eyes, and realized that she was looking at Anthony. He still had some of the IV tubes coming from him. His weak physical appearance frightened her. She now found herself staring her husband in the eyes.

A single tear fell from Aijah's eye. "Anthony, why didn't you tell me you had cancer?" She said in a weak, soft voice.

Anthony didn't speak right away. Seeing his wife's sad face, he had to force himself to fight back his own tears that were trying to force themselves out of his eyes. After he gathered his composure he spoke. "I'm a silly man, Aijah. I didn't know how to tell you. I felt that my life was over and I just didn't know how to tell you."

"Anthony, do you know how selfish of you that was?"

"Actually, Aijah I thought I was being thoughtful." Anthony said sensitively.

"Really, Anthony? How do you believe you were being thoughtful by abandoning your family and keeping such a grave secret from us?"

"Look. The day of our anniversary is the day I found out about the cancer. I wasn't thinking straight. In my mind all I knew was that I was dying and I said to myself that I need to help you all get used to me not being around..."

"What?! That is the most ridiculous thing I've heard, Anthony." Aijah quickly interrupted him.

"I know, baby, I know. When the doctor told me about the cancer, he gave me such a short life span I went into shock. But once we got everything under control it just seemed like so much damage was done, I didn't know how it would be possible for me to come back. I thought I lost you, especially when old boy came into the picture."

Aijah just shook her head. She couldn't believe what she was hearing come from Anthony's mouth. "All you had to do was communicate, Anthony. My love for you never left. I thought you didn't love me anymore. Honestly, today I was coming over here to tell you that I was filing for divorce."

"Really..." Anthony couldn't say another word.

"Yes, I thought it was over." Aijah says.

"But it is. I'm not going to recover from this."

Aijah jumped out of the sofa sleeper and sat right by his side. "Anthony, don't you know nothing is too hard for God? We're going to pray about this. You're going to church and we're going to have Pastor Richards pray for you and God is going to heal you. Do you believe? Do you believe God can heal you, Anthony!" Aijah yelled.

"My faith has been up and down for the past three years. But yes, I believe that God can heal me. I knew that when the cancer first went into remission. But when it came back that's when I knew you stopped praying for me."

189

Aijah then had a flashback. "That's why you asked me if I had stopped praying for you, huh?"

"Yeah that's why I asked. Then your little boyfriend started trying to edge me on and I was starting to get upset."

"This is crazy, Anthony. Can you imagine where we would be right now if you'd only learned to open your mouth and say what was going on?"

"Yes, baby, I know…"

Aijah kissed Anthony on his forehead and stared into his eyes. Right in that moment everything that she allowed and forced herself not to feel came rushing back in like a movie going in rewind. She cried before her husband over his illness. The fact that her marriage almost ended, and all the anguish that was caused because of Anthony inability to communicate frustrated her.

That day when she picked Jason up from school, the family spent time at Anthony's home. She relieved the nurse of her duties and didn't leave his side for the remainder of the week.

Chapter 27

Aijah kicked right back into wife mode after finding out about Anthony's chemo. Life wasn't easy, but she managed to juggle being a mother, her gig on the set of *Working Girls* and her other consultant jobs, and being Anthony's full time nurse. Aijah did take advantage of using the nurse that Anthony had hired to take care of him. They both worked together and she stepped in for Aijah when she had to step out. Thanks to God that Ahlesha was a rock star business manager, for Aijah was able to give Ahlesha full creative control while she took her hiatus to take care of Anthony.

Although Anthony was a strong man, his body reacted in the worst case scenario the doctors had ever seen. But Aijah was sure to stick by his side. The hours were long at the cancer treatment center where Anthony would go to get his treatment.

Aijah tried her best to keep him company by reading the Bible to him and bringing the portable DVD player for them to watch a movie on. Sometimes the scenes would be cute. They would both share a pair of earplugs as they watched the movie. Anthony would be in his hospital cot and Aijah would be sitting in the chair close next to him. She would get as close to him as she could and lay her head on his free shoulder. He would have one plug in his left ear, while she would have the other in her right ear. The scene was picture perfect, even considering the circumstances.

His body was beginning to break down and his veins were collapsing from the constant poking and prodding. Anthony was forced to get a picc line put in to help with the continuing of his chemo treatments.

Aijah was getting desperate while watching her beloved husband's condition slowly get the best of him.

"I'm glad Pastor Richards is finally getting the chance to come over to the house to pray for you." Aijah says while driving the car down the street and giving quick glances over to a weak Anthony.

"Yes, me too! Owww" He says as he raises his hand to his mouth. During the chemotherapy he started getting sores in his mouth. This was a common side effect that some cancer patients experience while getting their treatment.

"You ok, baby?" Aijah says in concern.

"Yeah, I'm good." He said semi-muffled. "I'll just be happy when the Lord heals me of this disease. I wouldn't wish this on my worst enemy."

Aijah gave him a sympathetic look. "Well the doctor said that your prognosis looks good, and I'm sure once Pastor Richards brings that healing power we're sure to see a miracle."

Aijah finally arrives at Anthony's home. She pulls into the driveway and puts the car in park. The nurse was waiting for them to arrive, so she stepped out from the front door to help Aijah get Anthony in the house.

It was a slight struggle to get Anthony's weak body out of the car and up the stairs to his bedroom. Anthony was so tired it seemed as if as soon as he hit the pillow he was fast asleep.

"Tonya, we will be expecting a guest soon. You can just send him right up stairs when he arrives. It will be our Pastor." Aijah says.

"Ok, no problem. Do you need anything else from me?'

"No, not that I can think of. But maybe you can bring up some ginger ale for later when he wakes up. You know how his taste buds have been weird lately. He says he's been craving ginger ale for the last month now."

"Ok, no problem, Mrs. Waters." Tonya said.

Aijah pulled the sheets over Anthony's body and sat down on the sofa sleeper next to the bed. Aijah was exhausted, too. Although it was Anthony that was physically going through the chemo, Aijah was feeling the effects just as well. She had late nights from being on the set, as well as rising early to take Anthony to his appointments.

As she laid there staring at her husband, she drifted off to sleep. However, it wasn't long before she was awakened by the chime of the doorbell. Her eyes popped open and she lifted off the sofa sleeper to go into the master bathroom that was in the room. She swooshed some mouth wash in her mouth quickly and made sure she didn't have any cold in her eyes.

Just as she was coming out of the bathroom, Pastor Richards was slowly entering in. As Aijah came fully out of the bathroom and looked up she put a smile on her face and walked over to Pastor Richards to give him a hug.

"Hey, Pastor! So glad you could make it."

They embraced, and then looked over at a sleeping Anthony. "How's he doing?" Pastor Richards asked.

Aijah had a drab look on her face. "Not good, Pastor. He really needs some prayer. His body is really breaking down from the chemo and he needs something to uplift him."

"Well alright, the Bible says the prayer of faith can heal the sick." He removed his jacket and then pulled out the blessed oil that he had in his jacket pocket. "Is it alright to pray for him while he's asleep?" He said inquisitively.

"Oh, yes, Pastor. He'll be out for a while. The chemo treatment usually has him out cold for at least four hours. So go right ahead and let the Lord use you."

"Well alright." Pastor Richard said.

He puts some of the oil on his finger tips and then anointed Anthony's head with oil. He then rubbed his hands together and then placed them both on Anthony's head.

"Father God, in the name of Jesus, I come before you on behalf of our brother Anthony. With the power invested in me I come against this disease, this deadly spirit of infirmity and take authority over it right now. God your word says that if there are any sick or afflicted among us that we should call upon the elders to pray the prayer of faith.

"Father, I believe that you have anointed me to lay hands on the sick that they may be healed. I believe, by faith and by your strips that you are healing Brother Anthony, even right now. I command you, spirit of infirmity, to loose your hold and be cast out, by the blood of Jesus."

Pastor Richards continued to pray with fervent fire. Aijah could feel the power of God fill the room as Pastor Richards prayed for her beloved husband. As Aijah stood to the side watching Pastor Richards pray she began to break out in a shout while speaking in tongues and declaring war against this disease that had taken hold of her husband's life.

"You come out devil even right now. You come to kill, steal, and destroy. But God says that it's not so. You will not be able to take this vessel, until God says that it's time. I command this body to respond to the name of Jesus and be healed in Jesus Name!"

"Hallelujah!" A crying Aijah exclaimed as she believed with all of her heart that God was going to completely heal Anthony.

After the Spirit in the room simmered down, Pastor Richards broke the silence of the quiet room. "Sister Aijah, you be encouraged. God is going to heal your husband, but you must make sure you take advantage of the time you have with him. Make up for the lost time that you two experienced during the tribulation."

"Hallelujah!! Hallelujah!!!" Aijah proclaimed as she broke out in a praise for the miracle that the Lord performed on her husband.

"Let me pray for you, Aijah." Aijah lifted up her hands in surrender, as Pastor Richards laid hands on her. "Father, in the name of Jesus, I ask that you watch over this vessel. Give her the strength that is and will be needed for this journey. We never know, nor can understand your reasoning, but by faith we know you make no mistakes. Show Aijah how to trust in your will and walk this uncertain journey you have before her."

"Amen." Aijah said humbly as she was grateful for the presence of the Lord dwelling in the midst of them.

Soon after Pastor Richards left the home and Aijah snuggled herself back in the sofa sleeper.

"You're ok?" Tonya asked as she peeked back in the room after Pastor Richards left.

"Yes, I'm ok. Thanks for asking." Aijah said barely looking up. She was so fixated on Anthony that she couldn't truly engage with Tonya.

"I felt that power all the way downstairs." Tonya said.

"Yes, I bet. Isn't God amazing?!" Aijah said as that caught her attention.

"Yes, he is. I believe that the prayers of the righteous will avail much and no weapon formed against will be able to prosper." Tonya said with power.

Aijah sat up in the sleeper and looked at Tonya. "You're a Christian?" She asked.

"Yes, ma'am. I pray over all my patients. Been keeping Mr. Waters on my prayer list ever since I got this assignment."

"Wow. Does Anthony know?"

"Yeah, he knows. On occasion I would sing this Aretha Franklin song, *The Day is Past and Gone* and he would always say that my wife would sing that song."

Aijah smiled. "Yes, my grandmother used to always sing that song. She wasn't much of a church goer when I was younger, but she said she always loved that song the way Aretha sang it. I sang it out of habit for a long time, until I got in the Lord and it started really meaning something to me."

"Well Mrs. Waters just know you all are in my prayers and I know that God is going to work everything out."

"Yes, I believe that, too. Just look at how much the Lord loved my husband. Just when I was ready to give up he made sure he had one of his soldiers here standing in the gap."

Tonya smiled and walked out of the room. She announced that she was leaving as it was the end of her shift. Aijah went back to staring at Anthony and smiled.

"The day is past and gone, the evening shades appear…" Aijah began to sang the soulful Aretha Franklin tune. "…O may we all remember well, the night of death draws near…. Hmmm, hmmm, hmmmm…" She began to moan the rest of the tune and smiling and falling asleep.

Chapter 28

Cough, cough. Aijah opens her eyes to the sound of Anthony violently coughing. "You ok, baby?" Aijah hops up in concern.

"Yes, I'm ok. I was choking on my ginger ale." Anthony replies back.

"Aww man, how long have you been up and what time is it? I'll have to pick up Jason from school soon."

"Oh, I've been up watching TV and listening to you snore for about an hour. And you have about another hour and half before you have to pick up Jason."

"Well you must be feeling good, you're over there making jokes." Aijah looked at Anthony strangely.

"Yeah, I feel great actually. I haven't felt this good since before the cancer came back. It's like I woke up and was feeling like a brand new person."

"That's that prayer that God anointed Pastor Richards to pray."

Anthony scrunches up his face. "Oh... I missed Pastor Richards? When did he come over?"

"When you were sleeping. You know how your chemo knocks you out, so I didn't want to wake you so I had him pray for you while you were sleeping."

"Well I don't know if the prayer is working, yet, but I do know I feel really good." Anthony puts a smile on his face.

Aijah looked at him and smiled back. Anthony continued staring and Aijah blushed. "What?!

"Yeah, I must be feeling really good because I'm feeling frisky."

Aijah blushed again. "Frisky, huh? So what are trying to tell me?"

"I don't know yet." Anthony laughed. "I'm feeling some kind of sensation but don't know if I will be able to do anything with it yet. But come on over here in this bed and let's find out."

The chemo took a toll on Anthony's libido. Surprisingly, Anthony has been just as celibate as Aijah had been during their entire separation. Although she had some guilt about her encounter with Calvin, Aijah was relieved that another woman hadn't been sexually intimate with her husband while they were separated.

Aijah hopped out of the chair and jumped in the bed with Anthony. They shared a passionate kiss and groped one another aggressively. Aijah hadn't kissed Anthony liked that since the last time they kissed when she tried to seduce him. She missed her husband greatly; she missed how it felt to be in his arms. The feeling felt weird, though, because his grip wasn't as strong as she remembered it to be, but she knew that was because of his weakened state.

Although Anthony wasn't able to rise to the occasion the couple shared a great moment of intimacy. Aijah didn't want to leave Anthony's side to go pick up Jason, but she knew that she had to.

She decided to stop at the grocery store to make a home cooked meal for her family. Anthony's appetite was up so he wanted a large soul food meal. Anthony hadn't eaten great since their separation so he wanted Aijah to hook it up. She made southern fried chicken, baked mac and cheese, baked spaghetti, and some fried corn. For dessert she also made him her famous peach cobbler and served it with some French vanilla ice cream.

Jason seemed so elated to be together with his mother and father. By now Jason was nearly five years old and he understood that his parents had not been together. However, he felt the love between his two parents and wanted to be right in the middle of it. They enjoyed family time for the rest of the evening watching movies and eating half a pan of peach cobbler.

The next morning it was time for Aijah to take Jason to school and she also had to be on set. She really wanted to take the day off to be with Anthony, but she was in the middle of production and she knew that was a no go.

She kissed Anthony good bye and toted Jason to the car to take him to school. After dropping him off she was quickly on her way to the set.

Once arriving on set she and Calvin immediately locked eyes. The two of them hadn't really spoke since Aijah found out about Anthony's cancer. Calvin had heard through the grapevine from Ahlesha what was going on, but he was waiting on Aijah to speak with him person-to-person.

She decided that she was going to be a woman about things and walked over to him.

"Hey, how are you?" She said to Calvin not really wanting to look him in the eyes.

"I'm great! How are you?" He said nonchalantly.

"I'm ok, a little overwhelmed right now. Ahlesha let me know that she told you about my husband."

"Yes, she told me, and whether you believe it or not I am sorry about his condition."

"Well thanks, that means a lot to me. But he's actually doing better."

"Ok, that great."

There was some silence. Calvin didn't know where else to take the conversation and neither did Aijah. After a few more seconds Aijah decided to break the silence. "So are we going to address this elephant between us?"

Calvin laughs. "Yeah, sure. Why not?"

"Why you have to say it like that? You act like we were seriously dating. Above all else we were friends. I would think that you would understand."

"For you we were friends, but I guess deep inside I was always hoping, well rather, waiting for more. I've been a very patient man with you." Calvin says slightly agitated.

"And I appreciate that about you Calvin. But honestly, I don't think it was ever going to happen. No matter how much I tried to tell myself that I was ready to move on from my husband, my love for him never left. Unfortunately, you were never going to win against that, Calvin."

"Yeah, I guess that's what I was in denial about. I really thought it was over between you two. I was waiting on you to just realize your marriage was over. At least it seemed to me that it was over."

Aijah had some bit of compassion for Calvin as she realized that he was really, really hurt. "Look, Calvin, I'm sorry. I really have no other words to say about this. I wish it was something I can say that would make this situation less awkward, but now things are what it is and we can't change it."

"I know, I know. Look let's put it behind us and move on. Let's also be real about it and know that we're not going to be friends. I know you from work and networking, and that's just how we're going to keep it... Ok?"

Although Aijah was grateful for Calvin giving her the easy out, the way things happened was painful to experience. She never meant to hurt Calvin, and she never meant for him to get that involved in her life. She never expected him to stick around as long as he did. He had even joined the church and really did seem like he was getting to know the Lord for himself. But like Calvin said, she had to put the relationship behind her and the two should move on with their lives separately.

After a long day on the set, Aijah picked up Jason from school and went back home to her husband.

Chapter 29

Over time, just as Pastor Richards said, God was healing Anthony. When Aijah found out about the cancer, Anthony's oncologist had ordered him to fifteen aggressive chemo treatments – at the time he was on number seven. After Pastor Richards prayed for him, within two more treatments Anthony had another scan and the doctor said that his cancer was ninety-nine percent gone. Although the doctor believed that his cancer was going into remission he wanted Anthony to finish his treatments to make sure that every bit of the cancer was gone. By the grace of God, the doctors only had to remove a small part of Anthony's colon and it was only a small nodule on his left kidney.

The aggressive chemo treatment was very helpful, but they both believed that it was the prayer that was really the reason Anthony was making such a quick recovery.

As soon as Anthony was well enough to go back to work and life was returning back to normal, Anthony decided to move back to the family home and he moved out of the apartment loft. Aijah was sure to do as instructed by the man of God. She was enjoying every bit of her recuperated husband.

In a year's time, they went on a trip to Disney World and took a few more family vacations. Aijah and Anthony were acting like newlyweds as they were definitely making up for the lost time every chance that they got. Because they shared such a special story Anthony suggested that two renew their vows in a private ceremony at the church.

They only invited about fifty guests; the guest list consisted of their close friends and family that knew their story and was happy that God had put their union back together. Everyone knew that they would be witnessing a beautiful miracle that God had performed on this couple. Anthony even renewed his faith in the Lord and rededicated his life back to God.

"You look so beautiful." Ahlesha said with tears in her eyes as she looked at her friend in her lovely white dress.

Aijah just stared at herself in the mirror. She flashed back at the moments that lead up to that day. Although she wished she could have avoided the separation and the cancer, she was glad that she made it through. She was happy that God had upheld her through it all and that she could still profess that she knew the Lord, Jesus Christ.

"Thank you, sister! And I thank you for being by my side through all of this. You truly are a true friend in deed."

A single tear fell from Aijah's eye as she looked upon her matron of honor in her cream silk bride's maid dress.

Ahlesha quickly grabs a tissue and dabbed Aijah's face. "Baby, don't mess up your makeup." She dabbed some more then grabbed a makeup brush to touch up the wet spot. "I really, really love you and I'm so glad you're my friend." Ahlesha said.

"Me, too!!" They both embraced in a hug.

"Ok. Now let's get out here to this sanctuary so I can see my man and we can renew these vows."

They get to the doors of the sanctuary and Ahlesha signals to the church wedding coordinator to start the processional music. The song that played was a gospel song by John P. Kee from the early nineties called, *I'll Be Your Everything.*

"I promise I will be there for you always, always. And you I'll receive on that day..." The lyrics sang as Ahlesha and Aijah came separately down the aisle.

Anthony cried as he saw his bride come down the aisle, and Aijah did too, as she smiled back at him. She was actually happy to have a wedding because the first time they got married they just stood before Pastor Richards one Sunday afternoon and got married before the congregation. So Aijah was happy to have her special day that she would always remember with her husband.

When she reached the end of the aisle to Anthony he extended his hands out and pulled his bride by his side.

Pastor Richards greeted the couple and went through his speech about marriage and the importance of God being the root and glue of a marriage.

"With the uncertain journey that love and marriage has to offer, you can't go in unequipped without the covering of God. You will need God to lead and guide you down every road that you will meet on this journey of marriage."

Everyone was shaking their heads in agreement with what Pastor Richards was saying.

"Now I understand that the bride and groom have prepared their own vows." Anthony and Aijah nod their heads. "Well I give the ceremony over to you two."

Anthony goes first. He looks passionately in her eyes and begins to speak. "To my beautiful wife, whom I love and cherish with all my heart, you have shown me that the love of God truly covers a multitude of sins. You are my virtuous woman, and I promise to treat you according to your priceless worth and be the man of God needed to love you as Christ loves his church, for as long as we both shall live. Give me the honor to continually make you happy for the rest of your life."

Aijah had a river of tears flowing down her face. There wasn't a dry eye in the sanctuary. The love that was being displayed touched everyone's heart.

Aijah proceeded to speak her vows. "To my handsome husband, whom I love and cherish with all my heart, whom God has shown me to never to give up on. Whom I know that I forever am your rib and belong to you as long as we both shall live. You are my lord and I promise to continue to allow the love of God to live richly in my heart that I may honor you as the man God made for me. Give me the honor to continually make you happy for the rest of your life."

After they finished their vows, Pastor Richards took back over the ceremony; he went over the usual ceremonial language that pastors speak when marrying couples. He said a prayer over the couple and then presented them before the audience. "With the power invested in me, I know pronounced you man and wife, again, you may kiss your bride."

Aijah and Anthony engaged in a very passionate kiss; the crowd went wild as they cheered excessively for the couple's nuptials.

The couple and their guest then headed off to their intimate reception, and then as expected off to their honeymoon. They enjoyed a full week in Paris, as this was a place that Aijah had always wanted to go. And with their fairytale love story it was only fitting that they be in the city of love.

Aijah really enjoyed herself in Paris with her husband. They did the sightseeing tours and ate at some very fabulous restaurants – they enjoyed one another to no end and hated that their honeymoon was over when it was time to come back home. Aijah just knew that the life ahead of them would be nothing but bliss.

Chapter 30

"We lay our garments by, upon our beds to rest; so death shall soon disrobe us all of what is here possessed." Aijah, dressed in all black with a bulging belly, sang the soulful Aretha Franklin song.

The Lord had made her strong, and she had the strength to keep her composure and sang the song her husband enjoyed hearing her sing around the house. There wasn't a dry eye in the funeral.

God had given Aijah and Anthony two and a half blissful years of making up and putting their marriage back together. Everyone was shocked to find out that his cancer had come back so aggressively that in the matter of two months it metastasized throughout his entire body. When the cancer came back Anthony didn't want to fight. He didn't know why God had allowed it to come back, but he had made peace with his life and allowed the Lord to have his way.

Aijah realized that the day Pastor Richards came to pray for Anthony that God was preparing her for Anthony's death. She was glad that she was obedient and cherished the time that she had with her husband.

"Lord, keep us safe this night, secure from all our fears; may angels guard us while we sleep, 'til morning light appears." Aijah finished singing the soulful hymn as the tears that flowed down her face dripped from the edge of her jawline.

She was quiet for a moment then she spoke. "I want everyone to know that God doesn't make any mistakes. God knows everyone's time limit on this earth. Anthony's time was up. Do I wish I had more time with him? Yes. But God knows better. I know some days will be good days, and then some days will be bad. But what I do know is that these last two and a half years that I've spent with my husband was the best time throughout our entire marriage.

"This definitely has taught me a lot about marriage and life. Simply. It's short and if you don't make the best of it you'll end up regretting a lot of things. I made the best of my marriage. Anyone that has any type of relationship that is worth holding on to, I encourage you to make the best of it. Get a relationship with God, and never let go of his hands. God bless."

Aijah stepped down from the podium as she could feel her emotions starting to get the best of her. She was met by a crying Ahlesha who was hurting for her friend. Aijah had been through a lot, and through it all she still remained strong. She remained a solid rock, being able to show her human side, yet trusting in the Lord. Ahlesha didn't know what to do for her friend but just be there in her presence in case she needed her.

The funeral went on as scheduled, Pastor Richards gave a heartfelt eulogy and ministered to the people about their salvation. Pastor Richards' eulogy turned into a sermon. Aijah was shouting "Amen" in agreement with the way he was taking the funeral. She didn't mind that if they had a little church. She knew that the people's salvation was more important than her grief – grief can be cured, but eternity was forever. After Pastor finished with his sermon the choir gave Anthony a going home song, popular Tramaine Hawkins song, *Goin' Up Yonder.*

"If you want to know, where I'm going? Where I'm going, soon. If anybody ask you, where I'm going? Where I'm going, soon. I'm goin' up yonder, I'm goin' up yonder, I'm goin' up yonder, to be with my Lord..." The choir sang so richly that the entire building was singing along.

The pallbearers took their places along side of the casket and carried Anthony's body to the hearse. With her friend on her left side and Jason's tiny hand in her right hand, she walked out the church knowing that she was going to lay her beloved husband to rest.

She got in the black standard limousine and sat down. She began to hum that Aretha Franklin tune and she smiled. She smiled at all the thoughts she had of Anthony – she didn't allow herself to think about the bad times, the separation, or the cancer, but of the good things. She was reminded of the Bible verse in Philippians chapter four that said to think on true, honest, pure, lovely, and praise worthy things.

God has blessed her with another baby that was on its way into the world, and she had a beautiful son that looked just like his father – who was every bit like him. She wouldn't let those sad thoughts creep into her mind. She began to hum a little louder. But Ahlesha, sitting close by, could feel the underlying pain.

They finally arrived at the grave site. The funeral goers all piled out of their cars and gathered around the burial. Pastor Richards said a prayer and proceeded with the famous burial sayings, "Ashes to ashes, dust to dust..."

As the casket lowered into the ground Aijah tossed a bouquet of twelve dozen roses into the plot. As she stood there knowing that the day would soon end she fell to her knees. She stared at that casket without blinking, but tears slowly flowed from her eyes. She didn't sob, she didn't become hysterical, but everyone could see the pain and mourning of the loss of her beloved husband. Jason could feel it too because he looked at his mother and began to cry.

Aijah snapped out of her daze and realized that her son needed her. She wiped the tears from her eyes, looked at her baby, and hugged him. "Ok, my baby. Don't cry. Mommy was just saying good bye."

She stood up, grabbed her baby by his hand, started humming the Aretha Franklin song, again and walked back to the limousine.

Chapter 31

Life began to get back to normal for Aijah. It had been two months since the funeral. Her grief was not in her thoughts as much as it was from the day of the funeral. She resumed her duties at the spa and was blessed to be able to be on a third season of *Working Girls.* Aijah was also asked to work on a new movie that was coming out and she found herself traveling back and forth to Los Angeles to consult.

Aijah didn't miss a beat as she knew staying busy was the only thing that would keep her sane. Ahlesha was worried at first that her friend was going to have a nervous breakdown at any moment, but Aijah proved to her that she was grounded in God and that she was going to be alright.

Calvin also managed to check in on Aijah every once in a while, but they continued to remain friends at a distance. Aijah was more so focused on building her brand and being a mogul in the fashion and spa world. She was also getting many opportunities to share the gospel with a lot of the people she was coming in contact with. She was learning to make the best of her time and the new friends that she'd made along the way.

Many doors were opening up for Aijah and she didn't want to let life stop her from moving along on the train. She was also using her connects to bring some very high-profiled people to Temple of Emmanuel. She was working more in the ministry and helped with a lot of the behind the scene operations in the church.

Posh Studios was becoming such a household name that Aijah and Ahlesha opened a second location in Chicago, and expanded the brand to Los Angeles after spending some time there. The New York City location was continuing to flourish and everything seemed to be on the up and up.

As usual, Aijah was sitting at the front desk in the spa looking over the appointment book when Ahlesha came over to her. "Hey girl, I want to go out for lunch today. You want to join me?"

"Yeah, sure. I need to go downtown anyway, so let's make it a shopping and lunch date." Aijah replies.

"Oh, you know I'm always up for a little retail therapy."

Aijah laughs out loud. "Girl, you're always doing retail therapy."

"I know, right. Sean is going to kill me when he sees the American Express bill from last month." They both laughed.

"Hey, I meant to tell you. Last week when I was coming from the set I thought I saw a familiar face. But wasn't sure because it has been so long since I've seen her."

Ahlesha frowned up her face trying to figure out who Aijah was speaking of. "Girl, who?"

"Guess..." Aijah said raising her eyebrows.

"Girl, I don't know, who? Just tell me."

Aijah paused for a moment. "Ebone!" She blurted out.

Ahlesha gave Aijah a side-eye and tilted her head. "You thought you saw Ebone? Are you serious?"

"Yes, I am. Very serious. But like I said I wasn't sure because it's been so long since I've seen her. Besides, I wasn't about to run up to her and be like, 'aww, Ebone is that you?' You know the girl didn't care that much for me."

Ahlesha laughed. "That is crazy. I do wonder how her baby is doing sometimes, though."

Aijah gave a smirk and then gets up from her seat. "Ok well let's get ready to get out of here. I don't want to hit that lunch time traffic on our way downtown."

"Ok cool. Let me run to the bathroom and then get my purse."

The ladies start to prepare themselves. Aijah cleans up a few receipt issues with some of the nail technicians and then grabs her purse. Aijah comes out of her office and closes the door, Ahlesha comes to meet her at the office door. As they laugh with one another making small talk and starts to walk toward the front of the spa.

They hear the door chime signaling that a customer has come through the door. They both look up and then stop right in their tracks.

This dark chocolate skinned, small framed woman walks in with her long Hollywood sew-in, Gucci bag, and designer attire. She looks around the shop until she plants eyes on Aijah and Ahlesha.

"Speaking of the devil." Aijah says.

Ahlesha couldn't say a word. Aijah grabs Ahlesha by the arm and pulls her up closer to the front of the spa.

"Well, well, well. Ebone! Long time no see." Aijah says snarky.

"Wow, ladies. I've been hearing so much about this place I just had to come in and check it out." Ebone says.

Ahlesha was still speechless as she was now folded her arms and looking Ebone up and down.

"Well, what do you think of Posh Studios?" Aijah says.

"It looks very nice and high-end. Is there any way you all can fit me in your appointment schedule?" Ebone says somewhat mockingly.

Aijah laughed. "Okay, here we go with this charade." She says mumbling under her breath as she grabs the appointment book. "Sure, let me see what we have available."

Ahlesha and Ebone continue to stare at one another without saying a word.

If you can think it,
God can make it happen.

Young Dreams Publications
www.youngdreamsbig.com

Check out other titles from author, Ty Waller.

Available in e-book & paperback.

Also check out POSH ANNOUNCMENTS, a boutique graphic design company by Young Dreams Publications. www.youngdreamsbig.com

www.ingramcontent.com/pod-product-compliance
Lightning Source LLC
Chambersburg PA
CBHW022043240626
47154CB00007B/2546